Into The Fire

ISBN: 0-9856-6792-3
ISBN-13: 9780985667924

Into The Fire

Book 1: The Survival Series

Travis Wright
Edited by Hannah Heimbuch
Illustrated by Melanie Noblin

Dedication

This book is dedicated to:

My mother Sheryle who taught me that I could do anything as long as I believed I could and didn't give up.

To my wife Candace, who is the love of my life. You have stood by me through the good and the bad. I wouldn't be where I am today without you baby!

"The power of our human spirit to survive / explore is unparalleled. We decide to continue on life's journey until all hope seems lost or our bodies not minds give up. Dreams can come true because we believe that they can. We possess the very ability to overcome any challenges. We all have the capacity to push ourselves, physically, mentally, and emotionally, as well as spiritually."

Anonymous

Chapter One : Confined Space (The Future)

"Billy, hey, Billy."

"What now?"

"What day is it?"

"Day 463," said Billy.

"No like is it Monday, Tuesday or Wednesday?"

"It's Saturday Carl."

"I'm going crazy. How much longer do we have to stay down here?"

"As long as we keep getting these strong radiation readings, according to Steve," said Billy.

"Hey Miranda."

"What Carl?"

"You want to play hide and seek?"

"No Carl I don't."

"Why not?"

"Because, Carl, there are only ten rooms and nowhere to hide. Look, this bunker is getting to all of us and if we want to live, we are going to have to deal with this for as long as we need to. Now go and find something constructive to do."

Deep down Carl knew all of this, but had to keep it as real and exciting as possible. Being stuck 50 feet underground with 13 other people for years had been a possibility and was now a reality. When their parents were approached with the idea a few years back, they had thought these people were just conspiracy nuts.

"Well you got to be glad you're here right?" asked Billy.

"I really don't know anymore," said Miranda. "What kind of future can we look forward to? We have enough air to breath and the water will last for many more years, but what about the food stores? We planned on being here for five years; at least we have supplies to last that long but, what about the surface? Will we ever be able to go back up and enjoy the fresh air and sunlight? We don't even know if it's all still there."

"We need to stay positive; our parents will come up with a plan," said Billy. "Look, if it wasn't for them we wouldn't be here right now."

The thought of never seeing the surface again or dying down there had crossed Miranda's mind many times. *I can't be the only one thinking this,* she said to herself. They would just have to do their chores and learn their chosen profession, that's what she kept telling herself.

Carl, Billy and Miranda were some of the teenagers that were brought to Sanctuary One to survive the attack that threatened the planet. No one really knew for sure who started it, but a determined few planned on surviving it.

"How's the book coming, sweetie?" asked Karen.

"It's more like a journal," said Steve.

"Ok, how is the journal coming?"

"Well, these kids give me plenty to write about, that's for sure. I've been documenting the days as they pass and it hasn't been very dull since we locked the door."

"Well I still think you should turn it into a book."

"I'll consider it," said Steve.

"Remember Joe is having his monthly firearms instruction class at 1400," said Karen.

"I'll try to make it," Steve replied.

"You know we all agreed to attend each other's classes in order to keep our minds from wandering."

"I know, but I just want to keep writing."

"You can write afterwards. I'll see you there; I'm going to change my clothes. Last month I got oil all over my shirt."

"Ok, see you soon."

The thought of sitting through another class on guns, guns that Steve could take apart and reassemble blindfolded, made him sick to his stomach. "Blindfolded, that's it!" yelled Steve.

"What's it?" asked Joe as he walked by the common area with a load of firearms.

"I know this is your class, but what if at the end you have a competition with blindfolds?"

"Why would we do that?" asked Joe.

"Listen, everyone has become proficient with the guns, why not bring some fun to the class with a competition?"

"These aren't toys Steve!" Joe walked away smiling, but Steve couldn't see him.

The class was just the same as it always was, everyone yawning and ready for it to be over. "Ok," said Joe. "As a special request, today we will see who was really paying attention. We will be taking the weapons apart and reassembling them blindfolded." Steve looked at Joe and they both smiled.

"Ok, here you go." Joe passed out blindfolds he must have made. "You will not only be timed, but you will get a place and bragging rights once you assemble the weapon and perform a function check. Hands to the sides of your weapons and ready, go."

Everyone raced to take their Beretta 92 9mm apart. A few parts dropped onto the floor. They would have to be recovered before they could finish assembly.

One minute passed and Nate yelled, "Done!"

"Does it shoot?" asked Joe.

Nate pulled the trigger, "click," and you could hear the others groan. Karen was the slowest, five minutes it took her to reassemble. Steve was the third one done. "Ok everyone good job," said Joe. "That was fun."

"I told you buddy," said Steve. "I think we all need to bring some fun to our classes."

"I think you're right, that engineer we have is the most boring teacher I've ever had." Steve pushed Joe down the tunnel for saying that. They both laughed as they put the firearms back into the armory.

"Life used to be great didn't it buddy?"

"I think it still is," said Joe.

"No, I mean on the surface," Steve said. "We just do the same things all the time and everyone is going stir crazy,"

"I know what you mean man, but if it wasn't for you we would all be dead up there. I'm glad you talked us into this."

The sound of the air circulation fans could be heard starting up. "It would just be nice to hear birds chirping again, or crickets at night instead of the fans," said Steve.

"We will survive and go back up there soon," said Joe in a positive tone.

Chapter Two: Prepare For The Worst (Present Day)

"Things are getting worse out there. The economy is bad and we keep seeing more crime and fewer jobs. What will happen next? We keep hearing about the end of the world. They've been talking about this stuff for decades now," said Steve.

"At least we have jobs Steve."

"I know Karen, but I can't stop thinking about everything. Do I prepare for what I hope won't happen? Is it going to be an ice age, a solar flare or just hell on earth? I've been reading about all kinds of conspiracies. The Mayan calendar says 2012, but everyone thought it was going to be the year 2000, then 2003. Many think it will be zombies. Did you know there is ammunition now just for killing zombies?"

"Unreal," said Karen.

"The latest thing I've heard is that the federal government is building bunkers deep underground for the elite and rich. Maybe we should build our own Karen."

"What Steve, a bunker? Be serious will you, nothing is going to happen."

"Yeah well what if it does and we weren't prepared? We should at least check into it."

"You go right ahead Steve."

As the days passed, the thought of being helpless sounded worse and worse to Steve.

"Well Karen, I've been doing some more thinking about that bunker I mentioned the other day and I think we should pitch the idea to our closest friends."

"What Steve like an investment?"

"No more like a just in case. If we were to get half a dozen people interested, it would lower the construction costs and we could all share it if something bad were to happen. I talked to Joe and he said we should build a few of them and pick people with certain skills that would be handy in case we do need to go underground and start over one day."

"Joe is that friend of yours with all the guns, right?" Karen asked. "What, he doesn't have his own bunker already? Sounds kind of farfetched to me Steve, but you know I have always believed in you. If you think we should do this, then we should." With that, Karen opened a new bottle of nasty smelling finger nail polish remover and went to town cleaning off yet another color that hadn't lasted long before she was tired of it.

Steve started to make phone calls.

"Hello?"

"Hey Nate, it's Steve, can you talk?"

"Hey man, what's up?"

"Well, I was thinking and had this idea about building a bunker, you know in case everything really went to hell, and I wanted to know if you would want to help."

"Steve, are you talking about one of those doomsday bunkers?"

"Yeah, Karen said I was crazy at first."

"Not necessarily man, I've gotten emails about those things. You can survive anything as long as you build it right."

"So you want to help then?"

"I think we should sit down, talk about it and come up with a plan, but I don't think it's crazy or far-fetched."

"Thanks Nate, I'll get back to you. Talk to you later."

Steve called a few more friends that he thought might at least listen and may want to join in the endeavor.

Bill was next.

After a few minutes of explaining, Bill said, "Count me in."

More phone calls were made.

"How about it Jake, are you interested?"

"I'll sit down with you guys and listen, but I'm not promising anything," he said. After some more calls later to Ray and Trevor, Steve had set up a meeting.

"Karen, I need you to go shopping for some finger foods. I set up a meeting to discuss the bunker idea next week," said Steve.

"People actually want to talk about the idea?" she asked. Steve just stared at her. "Ok, I'll go shopping."

Steve's friends showed up for the meeting the next week with their wives and girlfriends. "Ok, everyone this has to be kept confidential whether you decide to join us or not. We don't need other people knowing what we are doing."

"So," asked Maria, Ray's wife. "Is this like a secret meeting?" A few people laughed.

"Ok," said Steve. "I
 know all of this sounds like something out of the movies, but I think we should seriously look into the idea."

"We'll listen, since you bought the beer," said Maria. More laughter erupted from the group.

"I have read more and more about people building these things and I have to ask, what would you do right now if there was a major natural disaster of some kind right here in Billings?"

"Nothing like natural disasters really happens in this area, and that's why a lot of us live here," said Trevor.

"Ok, but what if?"

"We don't play the 'what if' game in our house," said Nate. Now people were laughing at Nate.

"You're cut off Nate, no more beer for you," said Steve.

"Time to switch to whiskey baby," Nate said to Kim, his wife.

"Now seriously, what would you do? Do you have a place to go? Susan, how many days worth of food do you have in your house?"

"I don't know."

"Can you guess?"

"A week's worth, maybe, but the grocery store has all we'll need," she said.

"That's what I was looking for!" said Steve. "None of you are prepared for the worst, I'm sure, and I want to get us there. Even if we never need a bunker, it will be there just in case. I even found a website called justin-case.com."

Steve made most of them think about what they did or didn't have in their houses. He had gotten everyone talking.

"Wow," said Karen as she walked up to her husband. "You really have their attention honey. You actually made me think about what we don't have here in the house too."

"I will continue to get more information, and if all of you are interested, we can have another meeting," said Steve.

They agreed to meet again to see what Steve could find out on bunkers. They thanked Steve and Karen as they left.

"Nice job buddy," said Joe on his way out.

Chapter Three: Research

"I'm finding more and more web sites dedicated to survival and how to do it, what you need," said Steve.

"Did you ask anyone else to help you do the research?" asked Karen.

"I want to do as much as I can to show them a plan that will blow them away and make them understand why we need to do this."

"Well, let me know if you want me to help."

"Ok, thanks." Karen meant well thought Steve, but she didn't really want to help. The planning involved was exhausting to say the least.

The information flowed out of the Internet for Steve and within a few weeks he set another meeting to show the group what he had come up with.

He had a power point demonstration, charts, graphs and diagrams ready to show them.

All of Steve and Karen's friends showed up for the meeting and were intrigued at the charts, pictures and information that Steve had gathered.

"This is unbelievable!" said Jake. "When you first called me, I had no idea how serious you were."

"I am very serious and I have some great news after the presentation." Maria was not causing laughter this time. She was actually asking serious questions about food, air and water. Steve showed them with pictures and graphs that the survival way of life was doable.

"We can store many years worth of freeze-dried food in a small space," said Steve. "Seeds can be stored for either growing crops underground or on the surface. Water was a concern until I read about a guy that built a bunker with a massive water storage tank on the side and just above. We can store enough water for years this way."

"How much water does one person need per day?" asked Maria.

"Excellent question," said Steve. "About a half-gallon a day for an adult depending on what they do, from very little to vigorous work."

"So, roughly one hundred eighty-five gallons a year," she said.

"Um," Steve had to look at his paper work. "Yes, that's about right. We would need a little more than a ten thousand gallon storage tank for fourteen people for five years. And here's something interesting, we can recycle water with the help of dehumidifiers and filters. We would have much more water than we needed."

"Alright," said Susan. "I know I'm not the only one thinking this. What about a bathroom and how do we store the waste?"

"Another great question," said Steve. "When you calculate the size of a large family and the size of a septic tank they have by the times they need to have it pumped out in a five year period, you can come up with the size of tank we would need. All the answers are out there, you just need to look in the right place. I have most of the vital information right here."

"Ok then, then how much will all this cost?" asked Trevor, a doctor with quite a bit of money.

"Well," said Steve. "A rough estimate would put the total cost of one bunker, with everything fourteen people would need for five years, at around fifty thousand dollars."

"Total cost?" asked Trevor.

"No each," said Steve. There were a few gasps and wows. "Listen everybody, it sounds like a lot up front, but this would have the best of everything we would all need for five years. Can you say that you could live on fifty thousand dollars for five years right now? Hell no, no one could." Steve could see a few people were ready to leave. "And I have saved the best for last," he said.

"We can use this as an investment. If down the road nothing happens, we could sell the bunker and actually make money. A lot of people out there would buy something like this, especially a fully stocked one."

People stopped putting on their coats to listen.

"Look, we can buy land for really cheap out in a rural area, and with a structure like this the land value would sky rocket. Please just take some time to think about all of this."

As crime rates rose, and riots over food and unemployment escalated, Steve and the others moved closer to digging the first hole. He had made them all think and start to wonder if he was right. More people were deciding to build. They selected a contractor specializing in hardened structures based on his knowledge, expertise and discretion.

The company was called Clandestine Construction. After the first meeting with the owner, the group knew they had chosen the right guy for the job and were convinced that building the bunkers was necessary. The company had built above ground and underground facilities all over the world. The group picked out one of the generic designs from a catalogue and modified it to fit certain needs and ideas they had.

They selected raw land on which to build the bunkers, and all those planning to live in them had an equal share of ownership. Corporations were set up with those involved serving as directors, so that everyone had to agree how assets would be split up. From land and construction costs, to supplies for the bunkers, all had ownership and responsibility.

They would need certain types of people in order to make the plan work for each bunker. A dentist, doctor, engineer, carpenter, mechanic and a survivalist or military man were a few of the vital specialists. Some of the group already fit the bill for these areas. Now, how to convince others to join? Steve was an engineer so he would talk to some people in his field as would the others in their respective fields. He talked to James, a civil engineer, and he was interested. Joe talked to his friend Craig who he shot guns with at the range. Jake was another friend of Joe's.

Within a few weeks, there were enough people to fill three bunkers. Trevor was able to entice Gary, a surgeon, and Simon, who was more of a scientist, but had gone to medical school. Legal contracts were drawn up and the money was almost in place to move forward. A few people could not come up with the full amount so their friends generously offered loans. One couple had four children. This was a dilemma because they would take up almost half of one of the bunkers and would have to put in more money to be considered. Most were couples with no children or had one or two. The idea behind every bunker was to have people that could handle any situation that arose. People were chosen based on what knowledge or experience they could apply to being able to survive underground and back on the surface later.

When everything was finally sorted out and they were ready to proceed.

Chapter Four: Breaking Ground

It was time for the first bunker to be built. The contractor would clear the land and begin the excavation. A fence and a gate were to be built once the road was put in to keep strangers out of the construction site.

Equipment was brought out and material staged once the fence and gate were put up. The contractor had six employees aside from himself and they were good at what they did. The entire project was to be handled by this one crew. In order to not introduce outside help to the project, they purchased all the necessary equipment and everything was kept confidential. They even had their own cement truck.

The construction started on a warm summer morning and a few of the group showed up to watch. They would try to have someone from the group on site for as much of the construction as possible just to make sure it was done to their satisfaction.

As the digging got to around thirty feet deep for the first bunker, the excavator ran into solid rock and part of the hole had to be moved over to miss it. Come to find out, as the digging continued they saw it was a giant boulder and there was gravel all around it. It was probably left over from an ancient glacier that had carved out the valley, the owner of the construction company said. If everything worked out as planned, the water storage tank would be attached to the boulder and the bunker would be built beside it. This was encouraging because it would only make the structure more solid. The plan was to pour the base and walls and then dig the septic and leach field off to the other side as the construction continued.

Each bunker was comprised of three levels. The first level had the bedrooms and the main room, which was to be used as the meeting and entertainment area. The second level held the armory, medical center, bathrooms, hydroponics, gym, kitchen and dining area. The third level was the storage area, laundry and mechanical rooms. The septic tanks and leach field were below the bunker's lower level and to the side. In the mechanical room, they would put a small water treatment facility for handling the solid human waste and all grey water from washing and showers. This made the septic tanks more efficient by putting less solid waste in them. Treated solid waste would also be used for the planting of the hydroponics area and for the garden, to give the soil more nutrients.

The showers were built with spray nozzles to conserve water. You would spray yourself down, lather up, and then rinse off, just like on some Navy ships. This was Craig's idea, and it would greatly reduce the amount of water used for bathing.

The entire bunker system was built with reinforced concrete and steel and was sealed with Drylok concrete sealant. All three levels looked pretty much the same in the blue prints except that some of the rooms were bigger or smaller depending upon their different uses. The structure was built to withstand a nuclear bomb detonating close by, or a large magnitude earthquake. The design was cell-like, with a larger room in the center and smaller ones on the outside. It looked like a beehive with its honey comb style. The octagon-shaped rooms were stronger than square or circular ones. The lid was reinforced concrete and steel, with a lead lining. The inner structure in each room of the first two levels was made mainly of wood, to give it a homier feeling inside.

A small cabin-like structure was to be built on the surface to hide what was below and to provide the entry point for the bunker. People would enter a room under the above ground structure and then access the bunker through a top hatch and spiral staircase that was wide enough to bring any necessary supplies up or down.

They were told by the contractor that total construction time would take about three months if everything went well. This was fantastic. Most of the group figured that it would take much longer. This gave the group the time to buy all of the supplies that were needed. Extra supplies that anyone needed or wanted could be brought in, but if an extended stay was a possibility then certain personal items would have to become community items. Everyone agreed on this, and purchased supplies for their rooms with what they thought they'd need. Each person with a specialty stocked their bunkers according to what they would need to keep life going if they had to move underground. Most of the group was having fun and found the whole thing interesting.

The project was to be completed by the middle of August. At that point, they could start to stock the rooms with all the supplies they'd collected. It was agreed to go as a group to bring items into the bunkers. With more people, they could accomplish more in a short time. Not everyone's schedule allowed for a lot of time to dedicate to the project.

About a month after construction was finished, just about everything was in place. Some of the plants for the bunker's hydroponics room were kept in the cabin on the surface for the time being so they wouldn't die. The plan was that if the bunkers were needed to escape a natural disaster or some other catastrophe, then everyone would show up with suitcases and enter the bunker. At that point, all the plants and any other supplies would be brought down and they would lock the vault door and then unhook the umbilical that exchanged air from the surface with the NBC filtration ventilation system, if that was necessary.

Plans had been drawn up for every scenario. What if some of the occupants didn't make it to the site before they needed to lock the doors? What if they forgot something important? What if this, what if that. All the systems they had in place from the battery banks to the electrical and plumbing were scheduled for testing once a month. They decided to have oxygen tanks to supplement the air made by the plants if O_2 levels dropped. They could also use the tanks if they needed some fresh air once in a while and the umbilical from the surface had stopped working, or if they didn't want to use it for some reason.

In order to make sure they had enough oxygen to breath in the sealed environment of the bunkers, they had to make sure they had the right ratio of oxygen being produced and carbon dioxide being exchanged by plants and the filtration system. They had a mixture of plants that needed little light to survive, like peace lilies, cast iron plants, Chinese evergreens and African violets. These different plants would be positioned around the bunker to provide the best flow of new oxygen along with the duct and fan system that went from the hydroponics room, through the lowest floor, and then back up the levels to circulate. They would also grow algae in tanks to maximize oxygen production. The bunker, when taken off its umbilical cord from the surface, was to be self-sufficient. With the flow room of waterfalls turning into electricity to be stored in the battery banks and the solar panels that absorbed the energy from the lights inside they had all that they would need. There were of course redundancies for everything. They were taking no chances. Though the stationary bikes they would ride for exercise didn't produce much energy, even those were hooked into the battery banks. Each room had a purpose, from the living quarters to the armory. They had everything covered. Being underground, the temperature would be kept even easily, given all the insulation and the radiant heat from the floors.

After everything was complete, the group members slated to occupy other bunkers in the later construction phases came by to see the finished product of the first one. Most were amazed at how it turned out. The people in Sanctuary One had given some of them ideas for their bunkers too. They were all to be built structurally the same, but the people that would stay in them customized the insides.

Each bunker was built in phases. When the excavation was done for one, the equipment was moved to the next site, and so on. All three were done by mid October.

Everyone involved was asked to not even talk about the projects outside of the group. None of their children would know what had been built.

"Loose lips sink ships," said Joe on a few occasions.

They were to be kept secret for many reasons. If nothing ever happened and the investors wanted to sell down the road, all would have to agree. If others around town knew then it might not sell as easily. A time limit of ten years was set for this to happen. It was considered an underground, ten-year investment. If the group needed to use them for any reason, they wouldn't want other people to try to get in, compromising the stability of everything they'd built. They were designed for fourteen people to live in for five years. It was an ecosystem that would die if it was tampered with once removed from the umbilical.

As a precaution, each bunker was built a few miles apart from the others. Considering the uncertainty of what might take the owners underground, it was considered a good idea by most of the group.

A separate bunker was built into the side of a mountain close by the few people that could afford it. It was carved out of the mountain and reinforced with steel beams and concrete. This bunker housed many more supplies from clothing to equipment, power tools, vehicles, ATVs and fuel. It was not designed for people to occupy it. The bunker had no life supporting systems, which made it cheaper to build and allowed for more items to be purchased and stored. The entrance was concealed by newly planted trees and shrubs. Once a person got past those, it looked like a large cave entrance with big metal doors covering the main wall. The items inside were things that would be essential in a post-war or apocalyptic world in order to rebuild and survive. The thought of everyone involved was that if they were building bunkers, then they better have everything else they might need too. Craig spearheaded that project and brought many items in that most were not aware of.

Chapter Five: Escalation

Winter was closing in and the surrounding mountains' snow lines were dropping closer. The building of the bunkers had prompted most of the people to upgrade what they had at their own homes too. Go bags and containers were staged in a specific area to be picked up and taken in a moment's notice. If they just had a big storm and electricity or gas or both were knocked out for a while, all were prepared to cope.

Nate didn't like to watch the news, because it was always the same stuff on a different day. After hearing from more and more people that tensions were continuing to rise in the Middle East again and the new leader of South Korea was out to make a name for himself, he started to watch more and relayed the information to everyone in the bunker group.

It was decided that mock drills should be done to see how long everyone would need to get together, enter the bunkers and lock them down. With everyone coming from different areas to converge on their bunker, these drills seemed necessary. The first one was done on a Saturday when everyone was at home. Most people took an average of forty-five minutes to get from home to their destinations and lock down. They also organized a drive from everyone's work to home plus load up time, so they could be prepared for that scenario. The group averaged one hour and twenty minutes.

Steve, Nate, a few others and of course Joe and Craig had their vehicles packed and ready to go with the other items they would want to bring with them if they ever needed to ever occupy the bunkers. Others thought they had what they needed in the bunkers already and still others figured they could just pack up at the time of emergency and then leave.

"I never did ask you but, what made you decide to do all of this?" Karen asked Steve one night.

"I don't know, I just had this strong feeling to look into the real possibility of a disaster and wanted to be prepared. People say that God talks to them, but this was different. I can't really explain it to you any better."

"Are you saying that God was talking to you?" asked Karen.

"Don't look at me like that. I said it was different, I don't know, it was just this strong feeling I had."

"Ok, I was just wondering. I think it's a good thing. At least we have a real investment, unlike the stock market. You know how much money we have lost in just the last year alone," said Karen.

"I know and you're right, we have a real investment that we can see and touch."

The weeks went by and those turned into months and the same troubling things were broadcast all over the TV. More riots in different countries. The world was being turned upside down. Church groups were continually talking about an impending apocalypse.

Winter was in full swing and it seemed like everything was getting more expensive by the day. Gas prices were now over $6 a gallon. Everything at the grocery store was getting more expensive and there was less and less stocked on the shelves. Mortgage foreclosures were rising again. Inflation was on the verge of hyperinflation. Tensions were critical in the whole Middle East region too.

Every day on Wall Street was another day in the red. A meeting was set up between everyone in the bunker group, as they called it, to discuss the current events that were taking place around them.

Everyone met at Gary's house. He was one of the doctors that they brought in and the wealthiest of anyone in the group. He had the biggest house and it worked great for the meetings since there were thirty of them now, minus the kids.

"Ok," said Gary. "Does anyone need a drink?"

"I'm sorry to get right down to business Gary," said Joe, "but I don't consider this a party so can you dispense with the pleasantries? We're here to discuss what is going on out there and decide when or if we want to implement 'Operation Underground.'"

"Operation what?" a few people asked.

"Ok, so it's not the best name, but does anyone else have a better one?" asked Joe.

"Listen up," said Steve. "Can we just focus on why we are all here please? The bottom line is that things are very bad and getting worse out there and Joe is right. When, not if do we go into the bunkers? Should we wait until riots start here or until we hear that nuclear missiles have been launched? Will we have time to get everyone together and inside before we lock the doors?"

"I think you need to slow down," said Nancy. No, things aren't great, but if anyone needs help, Gary and I are willing to help our friends."

"That goes for me as well," said Trevor.

"Excuse me?" said Nate. "What are you talking about? We are here to discuss the impending world collapse, not needing a handout. And none of us would be here tonight or have the bunkers if it wasn't for Steve, so can you just let him talk?"

"Well I have never..." started Nancy, before Gary cut her off.

"Let him talk, these men are right, this is serious honey."

"I know tensions are high," said Steve. "We need to figure this out together or everything we have done will have been for nothing. We need to stay in constant contact with each other. If something catastrophic happens, our cell phones will not work. Jake mentioned hand held radios. The main problem with those is that they have a limited range and need line of sight. Does anyone know of a better hand held that has greater range, say thirty miles? That would cover most of Billings. And besides there are few tall buildings in the way for line of sight."

"If you want to cover that distance," said Joe, "you would need a Ham radio and a one hundred foot antenna. The only other option would be to put an antenna on the top of a very tall tree right in the middle of all of our houses. This would cover most of us and we can get a real good hand held that would work in conjunction with the antenna attached to a relay point. It can be done."

"Ok," said Steve, "can you check into that?"

"Yes Sir, I can."

"That is the first thing. Now, about when to go underground." Steve said to the group. "None of us want to make a decision like this. We would all like life to just keep going on like everything is ok, but it's not. The reality is that a social breakdown could occur at any time. The signs are everywhere. So I propose that everyone just keep doing what you do every day. Nobody should go on a trip or out of the local area for now, unless things calm down out there."

"What about my mom?" asked Maria, who was starting to cry.

"My sister?" asked Kim. The room got very loud with questions and crying.

"Listen up!" Karen whistled loud and clear and it started to get quite again.

"We have discussed this at length," said Steve. "We can't bring anyone else into this or it won't work. My brother lives in California and I want him here, but it won't work. We decided that sacrifices would have to be made."

"But," said Maria. "I never thought this would ever really happen."

"None of us wanted this to come to fruition," said Karen, "but it might. Be strong sweetie."

"This is still up in the air," said Steve. "But just be even more ready than you have been."

Everyone started to get their coats on and make their way to the door. Not many were talking at this point.

Two days later, Joe had the radios ready for distribution and antenna in place. It worked great until around the twenty-six mile mark. Static was a problem, but most of the words could be heard. The radios were handed out, one per family. Now everyone sat back waited, and hoped that everything would be ok.

Chapter Six : Zero Hour

December twenty-first came and went, but nothing else did. The riots and food shortages around the world were making people even more desperate. The largest cities were of course the worst off no matter what country they were in and the United States was no exception. Martial law was implemented in many large cities and this made things even worse. People were trying to survive and feed their families, but getting killed by government troops in the process.

In smaller areas like Billings, things were only slowly getting bad. Most people had enough to worry about with the snow and trying to keep warm. Of course the shortage of food was a concern also. Not many celebrations took place on New Years. No fireworks were planned because they cost too much. The mood was unhappy almost everywhere a person went. The local hospitals had to have military and police guarding the entrances. With people starving and many homeless, they were going to places that still had food and heat. People were turned away by the hundreds at FEMA camps and hospitals.

North Korea was in a bad situation before any of the current tensions started, with a large portion of its food supplies donated every year from around the world.

The winter was taking its toll on the small country. Tensions were rising and people around the world felt the small country had been given enough. Troop build-ups along the southern border were normal when they wanted to flex their military muscle, but to pull troops back was odd. The reports on the news were sketchy. No one really knew what was going on over there.

The day that the world ended for many people was Sunday, January 13 2013. On this day, North Korea launched a massive strike at the United States. Dozens of nuclear missiles were launched from submarines at most large cities on the East and West coast and from the Gulf of Mexico. The attack was unprecedented in many ways. The attack from the sea was never expected and to only strike certain cities was considered strange.

The United States was forced to retaliate and launched ICBM missiles back at North Korea, which prompted China to strike the U.S. because some of the missiles were not as precise as they should have been and landed close to China. The fallout was substantial in southern China.

At that point, the bombs seemed to cease. The global fallout was severe enough to kill millions of people and much of the planet's wildlife. Vegetation in many areas was devastated as well.

These were some of the last pieces of news that any of the group got on their way to the bunkers in the early morning hours of that cold Sunday morning.

Then all TV and radio signals' went silent as the power grid went down.

Joe got the word out to everyone in time, he hoped. He wouldn't know if he reached them all for a long time. The call to get to the bunkers went out and then the radios were suddenly all static.

No bombs came near the small city, that they knew of as the families got into the safe havens they'd built. It was chaos bringing the kids into the shelter and locking it down. They had no idea what was going on or where they were. Everyone made it to Sanctuary One, but they had no idea if the other groups had arrived safely at their shelters.

"Nate can you unhook the umbilical please?" asked Steve over the radio.

"I thought we were using the outside air?"

"If we're nuked," said Steve, "Then I don't want to trust the filters if it's real bad. We will have plenty of air down here, now unplug us."

"I'm doing it right now and Joe is locking us in." Steve had gone down to the lower level to hook up the battery bank and start the airflow system.

"We are flowing," said Steve. Some of the women were putting the plants into their areas around the bunker. The hydroponics room would be one of the first things that they needed to get started. New plants would have to be started with the plants they already had. It would take time to raise them, but time was what they had most of at that point.

Some of the kids were crying and so were a few women. Steve asked for the whole group to gather in the meeting area.

"Please, have a seat everyone," said Gary. "We know you kids have questions and they will be answered, so please calm down."

Sanctuary One had four kids total with them, and they ranged in age from six years old to fourteen. Sadie was the youngest at six, and wasn't saying much at this point.

"What is going on?" asked Miranda, who was twelve.

"Steve you want to tackle this?" asked Ray.

"Ok, kids. This is what is going on. You know how it seemed like everything was going crazy out there?" asked Steve.

"Yes," they said.

"Well things are worse than you think."

"Where are we?" asked Carl who was ten.

"We are in an underground house that all of us adults built so we would be safe."

"How far underground?" asked Billy, who was fourteen.

"Well, the lowest level is approximately seventy feet below the surface. We have three levels and all of you will get to tour the whole facility. For now, I think we should all get settled and possibly get some sleep since it's only four in the morning."

Family groups went different directions to settle into their separate rooms. Steve, Joe and Nate were the only ones left and didn't really know what to say to each other.

"I know, I for one am glad you talked us into this buddy," said Joe.

"Yes, thanks," said Nate. "We owe you our lives and to tell you the truth, I think we all waited too long to come down here. We were hoping things would just get better. Where do you suppose the North Koreans came up with the capability to pull this off?"

"We may never know," said Steve. They slowly left to go back to bed.

Everyone woke a few hours later to an alarm going off. Beep, Beep, Beep! "What is that?" asked Gary as people walked into the hallway.

"Is that the oxygen alarm?" asked Nate.

"No, said Joe, that's the top hatch alarm. Someone is trying to get in."

"Can they?" asked Maria.

"There is no way they can honey," said Ray. "That door is bomb proof."

"Steve, can you still access the surface cameras?" asked Gary.

"It'll take a minute to bring the computer online."

Everyone went downstairs to the control room. Steve booted up the computer and went to work. Minutes later, he had it. "Here we go, and there we have a picture," said Steve. "It's a woman and two small children."

"Let them in," said Nancy.

Everyone looked at her. Nate asked Gary, "Is she drunk? I thought we decided on no alcohol?"

"No Nancy, we can't let them in and you know it. Go to the outside cameras," said Gary.

"Look, there is a man out there too. Where did that wind come from?" asked Nate.

"That's not wind," said Steve. "Keep watching." The scene outside was crazy and picked up speed fast. The cameras went black and the bunker shook as if there was an earthquake.

"What the hell happened?"

"That was the shock wave from an explosion, probably nuclear."

"Oh man, what the hell?" asked Nate. "The guy was just swept away right in front of us."

"My cameras," said Gary.

"Are you serious?" asked Nate. "The surface is gone man! Steve, will five years be long enough?"

"I really don't know yet. I'm sorry," said Steve. "Luckily with the Faraday shield, our electronics are safe and with the amount of concrete and lead lining we have on the top of the bunker, we should be safe from hard radiation as well. We will send up one of our balloons in a few weeks and see what the surface quality really is."

"How can you be so calm Steve?" asked Nate.

"I don't know man, I think because I knew this would happen."

"How did you know?"

"Why do you think we built this place?" asked Steve. "I had the strongest feeling I have ever had to do something and it worked out for all of us."

"How close was the bomb?" asked Gary.

"By the look of the shockwave, it must have hit Billings."

"Why bomb us?" asked Nate.

"The only thing I can think of," said Steve, "is that all the larger targets have already been destroyed."

"Are you serious?" asked Karen. Some of the women had been outside of the room listening.

"What did you hear?" asked Gary.

"All of it," said Nancy. "Are we going to die?"

"No, we are going to be just fine. We built this place for a reason and we are going to survive. Let's get some breakfast," said Steve. "I'm starving."

"Some of us have lost our appetites, thank you," said Nancy. Gary took her back to their room and the rest of them went to the kitchen to start breakfast.

"Steve, I want to know how you can be so calm," said Karen.

"I just am sweetie, now what do we have in here?" She was just staring at him as he looked through the food.

Joe came in the kitchen and asked if anyone else felt the earthquake.

"We sure did, and saw the detonation flash and shockwave of the nuclear explosion too," said Steve.

"We were nuked?"

"Yep, and we are safe."

"How can you be so calm?" asked Joe.

"That's what everyone is wondering," said Karen.

"Ok if I am so calm, how could you sleep through all of that?" asked Steve.

"I'm just a heavy sleeper I guess," said Joe as he shrugged his shoulders.

"Ok, can we just focus on breakfast?" asked Steve. More people started to enter the dining area to eat.

Everyone was sitting around the big table when Steve got up to speak. "I know a lot of you have had the worst night of your lives, but no matter what we will continue to survive and eventually rebuild our world. We have all lost a lot and wonder why this has happened. We are here for a reason; I know it with all my heart. I am glad all of you are here." No one else said much that morning.

As the days passed, everyone got settled and jobs were handed out. The bunker could almost run itself, but regular maintenance would have to be performed on some systems. They all had their specialties and had a place in the bunker for a reason. A network of computers had been installed with almost the entire world's data on the largest portable servers they could find. Just about anything could be accessed on them. It was like having your own Internet.

A cable had been considered in order to link the bunkers for communication, but the cost was high and it was agreed to put the money and efforts into supplies instead. Not being able to communicate with the others was a drawback, but they had to hope that the other groups all made it as safely as they had.

Karen had been a substitute teacher and set up a classroom for the four kids. "We will continue on with everything as close to normal as we possibly can," she said.

They all would learn the operating systems of the bunker and rotate out in order to maintain it. The kitchen, hydroponics, even the bathrooms had a rotation. Nobody was exempt from anything. They worked as though they were the last people alive anywhere, and for all they knew, they were.

Ray had been a contractor/handyman. He had helped design and build much of what they now had. Nate was a mechanic and good with his hands. Joe was the resident gun guru and a pretty good handyman as well. Gary was the doctor and a good thinker when it came to problems. Steve of course, the brains behind the facility, was an engineer. The wives in this group were mainly house-wives, but would learn many trades too. Maria had been a dental hygienist for a year and since they had no dentist, Gary and Maria had agreed to handle the job together. Maria had also worked in a salon while she was in college to help pay for it. Everyone fit in very well to make the new community work. The gravity of what had happened on the surface was apparent to some and still had others in shock.

Everyone was getting used to life in the confines of their underground home whether they liked it or not. They all owed their lives to Steve and knew it full well.

Chapter Seven: Aftermath

Three weeks after the bombs fell, it was time to send up a balloon. The information would be sent back through a transmitter until the balloon was out of range.

"What kind of readings would still be bad?" Joe asked.

"The amount of radiation is measured in Rads. 600 Rads or more is the worst, you will die very quickly. The lower amounts are still very harmful, but if levels continue to drop regularly then we should be ok in a few years," said Steve.

"Doesn't radiation last for hundreds if not thousands of years?" asked Nate.

"No, that is a myth for the most part. Look at Hiroshima and Nagasaki, well before all of this of course. Thriving cities were being built just a few years after they were bombed. There is much to take into consideration. How many kilotons was the blast, how close was the next detonation, what kind of weather was the area having, how strong were the winds? All of this has to be factored in," said Steve.

"So when can we go back up to the surface and start over as far as the Rads go?" asked Nate.

"As long as the levels keep dropping and we have less than ten Rads then we can slowly venture out. We wouldn't want to stay out there all the time until they dropped to one, two or none to be relatively safe. We will monitor everything on the surface with our Geiger counters and take our potassium iodide pills just to make sure we don't get sick," said Steve.

"What about suits?" asked Joe.

"Suits are a movie thing," said Gary. "You would have to be wearing a lead lined suit and then you wouldn't be able to walk because it would be so heavy."

"I didn't know," said Joe.

The balloon was sent up and everyone waited in anticipation. Steve described for everyone what would happen. The balloon would start transmitting information from the moment it was launched from the tube that had been put in for that very reason. It would relay everything back until it got out of line of site range of the antenna, or reached thirty thousand feet of altitude. The initial readings were just over 500 Rads on the surface and the average as it gained altitude was 400 Rads. With the particles on the ground, it was to be expected that it would be higher close to the ground.

"So it's real bad right?" asked Nancy.

"Well it's not great. It could be better or could be worse. We might just be in a pocket of radiation and will have to wait until it dissipates. We will send a balloon up once a month and monitor the situation," said Steve.

"We will still want to be careful when we do finally go up. A light dose like the one you would get from an x-ray is not really good for you," said Gary, "but prolonged exposure is worse. We all received doses of radiation from our cell phones, microwave ovens, TVs and many other things, but they weren't constant. Well maybe for Nancy on her phone." Nancy hit Gary, and everyone laughed.

"It sure would be nice to see what it looks like out there," said Maria.

"I think I can adapt a small camera onto the next balloon," said Steve.

"Yeah, but that's a month away."

"We only have so many of these balloons and less cameras, so you will have to be patient," said Steve.

Nancy was in charge of making the menu for the month from the food stores. She had to keep asking everyone questions about how to do it or what foods went with which meal. Karen and Maria had to go over everything many times before she almost understood. When Nancy went back to the storage room again, Maria asked Karen what her problem was. "She's always had housekeepers and cooks," said Karen. "This will be good for her, but we'll also have to keep a close eye on her."

Nancy came back out and asked, "Can you girls tell me what this stuff is?" They all went into the food storage room and Nancy pointed at several totes with blue tape on them.

"I'm not sure," said Karen, "Let's go and ask Steve."

They found him on the lower level on the computer.

"What you doing honey?" asked Karen.

"Just looking some stuff up, and what are you ladies up to?"

"I came across some totes in the food storage room and need to know what's in them so I can finish this month's menu."

"What color tape is on them?" asked Steve.

"Blue tape, so what's in them?"

"There are seeds for many different types of food and plants in them. We have salt and honey below those totes."

"Are we going to grow food?" asked Nancy. "I thought we had all we needed down here?"

"We do, but those are for the future on the surface. If you want, you can plant some seeds for some fresh vegetables in the hydroponics room. It will take a while, but it would be nice to eat fresh food. They'll help with the air supplies too," said Steve.

Nancy again asked for help from the other women regarding planting. They agreed and helped her. Joe didn't have much to do regarding the armory and the supplies in it for now, so he helped out where the others needed him. In between writing in his journal and working on the computer, Steve was busy helping everyone else, too.

With the adults staying busy doing things to maintain life in the bunker, the days went by fairly fast, and it was time to launch another balloon before they knew it.

Everyone crowded around the monitor to see what the surface looked like. Steve was soon ready to launch, and confident that the camera would work. He launched the balloon and within a few seconds, an image appeared and data started to pour in. The image wasn't very clear and the onlookers asked Steve to fix it. He told everyone to calm down, typed in some commands and turned some knobs. All of a sudden, they could all see the devastation. Most of the trees were on the ground or gone completely. What vehicles hadn't been destroyed by the blast, had caught fire and burned up. "My truck," said Joe, disappointed. "I really liked that one."

"Outside temperature is 29 degrees and rads have fallen to an average of 200," said Steve.

The balloon kept gaining altitude and they could clearly see what was left of Billings. Most of it looked like a wasteland and not many structures were left. They were silent as they watched.

"Anyone we knew out there, or saw on the street, is gone," said Ray.

"We will just continue on until we can go back out there and rebuild," said Steve. He had to try to keep everyone's minds from going to a bad place. "Movie night in the common area," he said.

It was Joe's turn in the kitchen along with Gary.

"Come on buddy," said Joe, "let's go see if we can make something good for lunch."

Everyone slowly left the room.

"What do you think about all this?" Karen asked Steve.

"Well, the radiation levels are dropping, but not as fast as I thought they would."

"What does that mean?"

"I'm not sure; this is all new to me too, so I'll have to search the database."

"Ok, just remember that lunch is being made."

"Be right there."

Steve kept searching and finally found a possible answer. He walked into the dining area a few minutes later and announced loudly that he thought he knew why.

"Why what?" asked Joe.

"Why the radiation is not falling as fast. The detonation was relatively close by, so that's the beginning of why it's higher. Second, it is still winter and it hasn't rained yet to wash down the blast zone and surrounding area. This is very good. If it had rained right after the detonation, then we would have high concentrations of radiation instead of it being dispersed evenly. Once spring gets here and it rains then we will have lower levels, I know it."

"But won't all the radiation go into the ground and make it so we can't drink any water?" asked Nate.

"Or plant any of the seeds we have stored?" asked Nancy.

"I suppose both of you are right," said Steve. "We will have to find areas that weren't affected by the fallout to dig for water and plant seeds for crops."

"You mean leave this area after we can go outside again?" asked Gary.

"Yes," said Steve. "We might have to leave this area."

The plan was to not launch another balloon for two months, to save on the few that they had left. With the information that they now had, it seemed the best way to do things.

Chapter Eight: Another Day In Paradise

"Why can't I take a shower every day?" asked Nancy.

"I have told you," said Gary. "We want to conserve as much water as we can and if we use too much too quickly we will run out and die."

"Well you didn't say die the last time I asked you."

"I have put more emphasis into the explanation, since the simple one won't do," said Gary.

"Well, you don't have to be mean!"

Nancy slammed the door and Gary said, "Yes I do," soft enough that she couldn't hear him.

"What's going on?" asked Nate as he walked by.

"Oh, nothing I can't handle. What are you doing today?"

"I just got done riding the stationary bike for an hour and I'm off to take a shower. It's the most exciting part of my day. See you around Gary."

"Gary!" yelled Nancy.

"What's wrong now?" he asked as he opened the door to their room.

"I want to ride the bike every day for an hour," she said.

"Ok, I'll see if you can get rotated in."

"No, I want to ride it and nobody else needs to."

"I will let everyone know honey."

"When can I start?" she asked.

"Tomorrow morning, I will make sure of it." Nancy hugged Gary and walked away smiling.

Water rationing had been implemented early on for bathing to make the water last as long as possible. With the recovery system and filters in place for bathing and cooking water it would last a long time, but making it last even longer was the best choice, especially considering the current radiation levels and not knowing if they would be able to find drinkable water on the surface.

"What's going on?" asked Maria as she walked out of her room the next morning. "Nancy is going to ride the bike for an hour," said Karen.

"Can she ride it for that long?"

"We are all going to find out." They walked down the stairs to observe the impossible. Nancy was having the hardest time underground out of anyone. She would constantly complain about her hair or her nails or how her clothes were wrinkled.

"How long has she been on it?" Nate asked Gary.

"Six minutes now."

"How long will she last?"

"I told her she couldn't shower unless she went the whole hour." Everyone was outside the room waiting to see how long she could last.

"Does she even know why she's riding that thing?" asked Ray.

"She doesn't care," said Gary, "as long as she can shower more than once every three days."

"This is great," said Nate with a smile.

"Stop it," said Kim. "What if that was me in there?"

"I would still be out here watching baby."

Kim stuck her elbow in her husband's ribs, earning a few chuckles from the rest of the group.

"Quiet down or she will hear you," said Maria.

Nancy kept going and made it the whole hour. No one could believe it. She walked out of the room dripping with sweat as everyone walked away.

"What's everyone doing here?" she asked Gary.

"Oh, I think they're just going about their duties." Nancy walked to the bathrooms to take her shower and Gary reminded her not to use too much water.

The rest of the day, Nancy was complaining about how sore she was and everyone just ignored her. She went to bed early that night.

The next morning, people started asking Gary where Nancy was.

"She is really tired, and sore," he said. "She's sleeping in today." Laughter filled the dining area.

"Well, at least she got her shower," said Nate. "So I guess we'll go back to the regular schedule then?"

Suddenly, the lights went out and the fans for the air circulation system stopped turning.

"The emergency lighting didn't switch on," said Gary.

"Ok, everyone just stay still and calm," said Steve.

"What is going on?" asked Kim, her voice trembling.

"You all stay here. I'll go and see," said Steve.

He left the room, found a flashlight and went downstairs. Steve reached the mechanical room on the lower level and found the two boys, Carl and Billy, sitting on the floor.

"What are you two boys up to?" asked Steve.

"Um," said Billy. "We were just looking something up on the computer and the lights went off."

Steve opened up the laptop cover, typed a few things in and the lights came back on. The air circulation system followed the lights.

"So, what were you looking up?"

"We were just looking," said Billy.

Steve motioned for them to come over to the computer.

"I don't have any porn on this computer or anywhere in the database young man." They both looked scared. "If you promise to never touch these computers again until you are properly trained, I won't tell your parents."

"We won't," said Billy as he nudged Carl.

"Uh, no sir I won't."

The rest of the adults came downstairs to see what Steve had found as far as the power outage.

"What are you boys doing down here?" asked Ray.

"They were looking up some stuff for school that they couldn't find on their iPads," said Steve, "and hit the wrong button. I'll password protect the main com-

55

puters for the time being so this doesn't happen again, but the boys told me they won't come in here again until they are required to."

"I want you upstairs now young man," Nate said to Carl.

"That goes for you too mister," Ray told Billy.

"Let's not do that again," said Karen.

"Agreed," said Maria. "Enough has happened already, I don't need any more excitement for a while."

"Don't be so fast to say that honey," said Ray as he winked at her. Maria grabbed Kim and walked upstairs.

"Why are men always thinking of just one thing?" she asked Kim. "The world has ended and he just wants to have sex."

"I don't know," said Kim, "but I for one don't mind at all." The women giggled as they walked down the hall.

"Gary, can you help me check all the systems and make sure everything is ok?" asked Steve.

"Yeah, I was pretty much done with breakfast anyway."

"Karen, would you mind reheating mine and Gary's breakfast and bringing it down here please?" asked Steve.

"You bet I will honey," she said with a smile.

"What is she so happy about Steve, if you don't mind me asking?"

"Karen is pregnant," said Steve.

"What?" exclaimed Gary. "How do you know and shouldn't I be telling you this news?"

"She took a home pregnancy test and it was positive. We were going to go and see you just to be positive, but we wanted to wait awhile."

"Why, might I ask?"

"We didn't want the others to get excited about air and supplies with another person down here."

"You know that won't even be an issue right?" asked Gary. "It will be eight months before the child is born and with such small lungs it won't use much air, and food won't be an issue for quite a while."

"Logically, we know all of this, but some of the others will need reassurance that we won't run out of anything," said Steve.

Chapter Nine: Genesis

Steve and Karen went to go see Gary for what he called a regular checkup a few weeks later. This is what he and Steve had discussed just to be certain.

Steve just sat in the corner as they discussed everything. Steve didn't like hospitals and would rather not be in the room. He was there to support his wife.

"How are you feeling Karen?"

"I'm feeling pretty good actually."

"This is your first pregnancy?"

"Uh, yes it is," she said as she looked at Steve. "Why would you ask that?"

"We all have secrets," said Gary. "I just want to get all the facts, that's all, and I am just being thorough." Gary examined Karen and found her to be perfectly healthy and noted so in her record. "Karen, I want you to take these prenatal pills."

"Wow, you came prepared."

"We knew that people would eventually have children," said Gary, "and yes we tried to be as prepared as possible. I just hope we thought of everything. We don't have some of the machines that I would like to have, but not everything was accessible to us."

Gary had started medical files on everyone as soon as they had entered the bunker. Some had brought copies of their records down with them, which would help him if anything came up.

All of the adults were asked to gather in the main room for some news the next day. Steve and Karen got up in front of everyone. He started by saying he was glad that all of them were here together, when Karen blurted out, "I'm pregnant!" There were a few wows and most got up to congratulate them.

Joe was the one to ask the hard question.

"Ok, what about the air and supplies for only fourteen people?"

"We knew that would be asked," said Steve. "With months before the baby will even be here, and after the birth with such small lungs, it would be years before additional air supply would even be considered an issue. We will have plenty of time to grow more plants to handle a larger volume of carbon dioxide. We will be fine, and we need to start rebuilding our civilization eventually and Karen and I think this will be a good start."

Kim walked up to Karen and asked if she could organize the baby shower. "A baby shower?" asked Karen. "You really don't need to do that."

"Yes I do," said Kim. "You can't have a baby without a celebration with a bunch of crying women giving you things."

The mood around the bunker was a happy one for days after the news. Couples and families went about their daily lives and tried not to think too much about what had happened to the world above.

"What are you doing?" Karen asked Steve one day as she walked into the common area and saw him sitting on one of the couches, writing on a tablet.

"Just writing a journal," he said.

"How long have you been writing this?" she asked him.

"I started a few months ago when we started talking about building the bunkers."

"I'm surprised you never mentioned it," Karen said.

"I haven't been hiding it," said Steve. "I guess you were never that interested in what I was doing until now."

"I'm sorry," said Karen. "What's it about?"

"Like I said, it's just a journal documenting everything, from since we started talking about constructing these bunkers, until today."

"Can I read it?" asked Karen.

"When I'm not writing in it, you sure can," said Steve. Karen walked away still glowing like she had been since she found out she was pregnant.

"We have babies," Nancy said as she walked into the common area one morning.

"What are you talking about?" asked Karen. "Are you pregnant too?"

"No silly," said Nancy. "I just came from hydroponics and the plants have sprouted. I am so excited," she said. "We will have fresh tomatoes, cucumbers, onions and..."

Karen cut her off and said, "I look forward to them also."

"Why don't you like me?" asked Nancy.

"I do like you."

"Then why do you cut me off when I'm talking and don't want to spend time with me like you do with the other girls?" she asked as she started to cry.

"I'm sorry," said Karen. "I didn't realize that I had hurt you."

"Well you did and I just want to know why."

"Truthfully?" asked Karen.

Nancy nodded her head yes.

"Well, it's because of how you are with people, like we are beneath you," said Karen.

"I don't think you are beneath me, I love hanging out with you girls and learning from you," said Nancy. "We are living in a different world now and we need to stick together.

I'm just having a hard time with all of this and I don't mean to make you feel that way."

"Come here and give me a hug," said Karen.

The vegetables continued to grow and were soon ready to eat. The girls picked the ripest ones and put together a fantastic dinner.

The table was full of food, as if it was Thanksgiving, and as the room filled up, no one could believe that Nancy was the one that grew the fresh vegetables.

"This is great," said Steve, "I knew you could do this."

"It's your turn next in the rotation for meals, and I expect the same types of meals," Nancy said as she looked at Steve and Gary.

There was laughter in the air as they sat down and ate the best meal they had had in months.

The next day Karen, Maria and Kim asked Nancy to join them in playing their weekly card game. Maria talked about turning an area into a salon where she could cut hair and the ladies would have a place to go to relax and paint each other's nails. The others liked the idea and agreed to help her.

The world was alive once again with happiness, at least the world they had.

Chapter Ten: Disrupted

The time below the surface was moving at a fast pace, everyone was kept busy so they wouldn't lose it. No one wanted to be down there, but it was obviously better than the surface.

It was summer time up there, the middle of June, which meant it was time to send up another balloon. Maria asked Steve if he was going to put another camera on the balloon so they could get a look at the area with all the snow gone.

"We have three more cameras," said Steve. "And I really don't want to use another one yet." Everyone wanted to see what the outside looked like now, so Steve relented and attached one to the balloon. They crowded around the screen as usual to see what was up there now that winter had come and gone.

Steve hit the launch button and about twenty seconds later they could see the data streaming back and a picture of the surrounding area. The temperature was only 34 degrees and they could still see a lot of snow on the ground. "Well, we have an average of thirty Rads," said Steve.

"Why is it still so cold out there?" asked Gary.

"That's a good question," said Steve.

All of a sudden the picture and data stopped. "What was that?" asked Nancy.

"Just a minute," said Steve, "I'll play the video back...I don't see anything. Let me slow it down some."

"How high was the balloon?" asked Ray.

"About three thousand feet," said Steve.

"Did it drift close to the mountains and pop?" asked Gary.

"There was very little wind and no trees, I will have to keep looking at the video and analyzing the data," said Steve.

Gary stayed in the control room to help but the others left the room to let them figure it out.

"At least the radiation levels have gone down to lower levels," said Ray, to anyone who would listen.

"You're right man," said Joe as he walked up behind him. "It's looking better all the time."

"What's the first thing you want to do when you get to go back out?" asked Ray.

"I want to feel the wind on my face and breathe fresh air."

"That sounds like something my wife would say," said Ray.

"Are you calling me a girl?" asked Joe.

"I'm just messing with you man."

"That's good, because I would have to tell you to meet me behind the bleachers after school so I could kick your ass."

"Don't hurt my man," said Kim as she walked up smiling. "You boys better be nice to each other."

"I challenge you to combat on the Xbox."

"You're on," said Joe.

The guys walked away to the common area to play.

Nancy walked up to Kim and asked, "Why were the guys acting so strangely?"

"They are extremely bored," Kim said.

"I see," said Nancy.

"Do you see that?" asked Steve.

"No, what is it?" asked Gary. "Can you enhance that? Is that a man?"

"I think it is," said Steve.

Both men looked at each other and then back at the screen. "It looks like he was shooting a rifle and shot the balloon down," said Gary. "Do you think he is from one of the other sanctuaries?"

"If he is," said Steve, "then he won't be alive for long and should know better. They know how deadly the radiation is and wouldn't shoot our balloon down either. I don't think he is from one of the bunkers."

"A survivor?" asked Gary.

"I don't know, but he won't last long out there."

Steve and Gary asked everyone to meet in the commons to discuss what happened to the balloon.

"What do you mean the balloon was shot down?" asked Karen.

"A man shot the balloon down? How could he survive out there?" asked another.

Everyone was asking questions at the same time and Steve just asked calmly if he could talk. They all stopped talking and let him continue.

"We can only guess at why he shot the balloon down and why he is out there. We won't be going out to investigate."

"Can he get in?" asked Maria.

"No, he can't, right Steve?" asked Ray.

"He would need a cutting torch or plasma cutter to get in and it would take him quite a while to do it," said Steve.

"We need everyone to stay calm and just keep doing what you have been. When the radiation levels drop to a less lethal level then we will go out and answer all of the questions you have."

"Joe, I need to talk to you," said Steve. People emptied out of the common area and Steve and Joe went downstairs.

"What's going on Steve?"

"What do we have in the armory that is non-lethal?" asked Steve.

"We have rubber shotgun rounds, why?"

"We need you to be ready to defend this place if for some reason it is attacked and whoever is out there gets in. Non-lethal will assure none of us get killed in the process. I would like you to train all of us in the use of the shotgun too."

"I would be happy to, that's why I'm here," said Joe. "I know the women will start to ask questions, so I have a better idea."

"What do you have in mind?" asked Steve.

"We all came down here with our specialties right?" asked Joe.

"Yes, we were all chosen to be able to handle any problem that arose."

"So," said Joe. "What if we all have classes once a month on our specialties so that any of us can eventually handle it all?"

"I like your way of thinking Joe. We can all learn from each other and mask the firearms training by teaching everyone."

"You got it man," said Joe.

"I will talk to everyone and have them put together a teaching plan in their areas of expertise. We can start the classes with you teaching the shotgun. We can run drills also as an excuse to have shotguns in each bedroom instead of just the armory," said Steve.

The thought of teaching a class made a few people nervous, but it was agreed that it was a good idea. "We shouldn't always rely on Ray to build things or Joe to be the only one that could shoot a gun," said Kim. The classes from Steve on engineering or from Gary on medical needs were going to be the toughest, but the need to learn from each other was agreed upon.

Chapter Eleven: Learning Curve

The first class was to be taught by Joe. The topic was the twelve-gauge shotgun.

Joe put a shotgun in front of each adult around the dining table. "Now," he said "And kids you listen close. Please do not touch the firearms until we get to that point in the class. I will use the dry erase board for the first part of the class and then we will get into breaking the shotgun down and then reassembling it. When everyone feels comfortable with that step, we will then move on to loading, unloading and clearing misfires."

Joe started the class with the four firearm safety rules and wrote them on the board.

> *RULE I: TREAT ALL GUNS AS IF THEY ARE ALWAYS LOADED*
> *RULE II: NEVER LET THE MUZZLE COVER ANYTHING YOU ARE NOT WILLING TO DESTROY*
> *RULE III: KEEP YOUR FINGER STRAIGHT AND OFF THE TRIGGER UNTIL YOUR SIGHTS ARE ON THE TARGET AND YOU ARE READY TO FIRE*
> *RULE IV: BE SURE OF YOUR TARGET AND WHAT IS BEYOND IT*

He then went through the parts with everyone using the diagram he drew on the dry erase board. As he covered each step, he asked if anyone had any questions. He answered them and went on.

"Who has fired a firearm before?" asked Joe. Most people had, by the show of hands. "OK, good, now who has shot a shotgun?" Only three of them had. "Alright, now who is not comfortable with guns at all?" Nancy raised her hand. "Thank you Nancy," said Joe. "I want you to tell us why you are scared or don't like them."

"Well," started Nancy.

"Go ahead," said Gary.

"My brother took his own life with a gun," said Nancy.

There was silence in the room.

Joe spoke. "It's not the gun that's dangerous, it's the person behind the gun. Your firearm is just a tool to be used just like any other. If you load this shotgun like this," said Joe, as he put a shell in the tube and then cambered it. "It is not any more dangerous than this knife," he said as he pulled the blade out of his pocket. He put them both on the table and asked Nancy which one was worse.

"They both are dangerous," she said.

"Wrong," said Joe, "neither of them is until we pick them up and decide to do something bad with them. Until then, they are just tools. If and when they are picked up and something good is done with them, like defending someone, then how can they be bad or dangerous?"

"Well, they wouldn't be," said Nancy.

"My point exactly," said Joe, "it's the person behind the tool that is good or bad."

"I see your point and I will try to be open minded with all of this," said Nancy.

"That's all I can ask. Now, who wants to take apart their shotgun?"

The class continued with disassembly and assembly of the shotguns the rest of the afternoon.

"I wish I could shoot this thing," Nancy said at the end of the class.

"When we get to go back into the world," said Joe, "we will shoot all of the weapons we have down here. That's right, we will learn about all of the weapons in the armory eventually." There were a few sighs, but most were looking forward to learning the other weapons.

"I want each couple to take a shotgun to your rooms with you and keep it in a place you can easily access it if needed," said Joe.

"Why do we need to have these in our rooms? Isn't that what we have an armory for?" Kim asked.

"Yes," said Joe, "but we will not always have them in our armory especially when we leave here. Just put it out of reach of the kids like above the door if it makes you feel more comfortable. Remember we had them in this class to teach them also."

"You have a point, but I would still feel better if they were locked up."

"Kim, do you remember the lesson Nancy learned today? Just think of it that way."

"I'll try, thanks Joe."

Steve was teaching the class the following week on engineering a bridge. Not many people were looking forward to that one.

It was decided that every week a class would be taught by someone else in the group on a different subject in their field of expertise, in order for everyone to learn more and to keep things from becoming duller than they already were.

The days lingered on and soon the summer that nobody got to enjoy was gone. "Can you believe we have been here for almost a year Nate?"

"Ray, it's only been eight months."

"Yeah, but it seems like so much longer."

"I know, but you're glad that you and Kim are here right?"

"Part of me says yes, but then the other part says what do we have to look forward to?"

"A brand new world," said Steve as he walked in on the conversation.

"So when are we going to launch another balloon?" asked Nate. "It's been more than a month hasn't it?"

"We don't have many left and I know, we haven't launched one since that one got shot down. We will again soon," said Steve.

A few days passed and Steve announced that he was going to launch a balloon without a camera this time because he only had two left. Everyone gathered around as usual and Steve opened the launch tube door. Rocks poured out, and Steve shut it as fast as he could. "Everyone get back!"he yelled. "Gary, get me a Geiger counter." Everyone else needs to get upstairs.

Gary came back from the storage room with a box and pulled a Geiger counter from it. Steve turned it on and put it over the rocks that had come out of the tube. "Barely registering, but how did they get in there?" Steve said out loud.

"The man on the surface," said Gary. "He must have seen where the balloon came from and filled the pipe up."

"Why would he do that?" asked Steve.

A meeting was called to discuss the possible threat. As usual, the room was loud and full of questions. Steve just stood there calmly until everyone saw that he was waiting, and they stopped talking.

"Alright, now that you are all calm," said Steve, "we can begin. Yes, the tube that we launch our balloons from is full of radioactive rocks put in there by an unknown person or persons."

Ray interrupted him and asked, "What are we going to do about it?"

"I was going to tell everyone, that we will no longer use the launch tube because we have no place to store the rocks and don't know if it will be filled back up."

"So," asked Nate, "how will we know when it's safe to go outside?"

"We won't, unless one of the other sanctuary's personnel come and lets us know it's safe. The three of us engineers set up a password using Morse code that would let us know that the person outside was a friend."

"What if they are compromised or tortured for the information in order for others to gain access to this place?" asked Nate.

"We will just have to be prepared for that scenario," said Steve.

A few days later in the early morning hours, the hatch alarm woke everyone up. Nate and Joe showed up with their shotguns, but no one else did. Joe told Gary and Ray to get theirs. They all assembled by the interior door and saw that Steve was already there.

"Four minutes," said Steve.

"Uh, four minutes for what?" asked Ray as he yawned.

"It took four minutes for all of you to assemble with your shotguns ready to defend this place. Not bad for the first time."

"You set this up?" asked Nate.

"Yes I did, and you should be glad it was only a drill. The next time it might be real," said Steve.

"It's not even four a.m.," said Ray.

"Would you say that to someone that just cut through the hatch to rape, murder and take what we have? Would you ask them if you can get more sleep first? Or say wait, I forgot my shotgun let me go get it?" asked Steve. "This is serious and I would hope that you would take it that way. Someone is out there right now waiting for us to open up and let them in so they can do just that. The world out there that we knew is gone, and they know that it's safe in here or we wouldn't be here. We need to be ready, because we can't stay here long term. We knew that going in. I am happy that some of you came here with your shotguns. That is the reason Joe and I had you take them to your rooms."

They all went back to bed, except Steve. He went down to the lower level to look up information on the computer.

"Honey will you please come back to bed?" asked Karen as she walked into the room. "What are you doing up?" Steve asked her.

"Are you kidding? Everyone woke up if not because of the alarm, then during the lecture you gave the guys."

"Do you think I was too hard on them?" asked Steve.

"No, you are right and they know it. You are our leader and you have been from the start. They all look up to you and believe in you. We know things will be hard once we leave here, but for now we don't want to face the truth. You were right in calling these sanctuaries. We all owe you our lives. Let's go to bed."

Chapter Twelve: Friend or Foe

The guys eventually apologized to Steve for being mad at him for waking them up for the drill. It was a good test and needed to be done.

One November afternoon while lunch was being served, Gary asked the group to be quiet. "What's that tapping noise?" he asked. The room was silent as people listened.

"That's Morse code," said Steve. They all looked at him. "I need everyone to stay here and be quiet please while Joe and I go to the top hatch."

The two men got their shotguns and loaded them with rubber slugs. They made their way up to the hatch.

"Do you think it's coming from the top, or the bottom hatch?" asked Joe.

They listened again and Steve said, "Definitely the top one." Steve turned on the Geiger counter. It showed no radiation readings so they opened the lower hatch that lead up to the surface one, where the cabin was or used to be. The air was stale and Steve still got no readings from the Geiger counter.

They listened carefully to the tapping and Steve said, "It's James, I know it."

"How do you know?" asked Joe.

"The code we came up with, he just asked me what the 'Uncertainty Principle,' is. My response would be Quantum Theory."

"Try it," said Joe.

Steve tapped on the hatch and then there was tapping back.

"What did he say now?" asked Joe.

"He said this is James and I have Jake from Sanctuary Three with me. We need to talk about the marauders on the surface."

"Then there are survivors out there?" asked Joe.

"Apparently there are. Let's go tell the others and make a contingency plan just in case this is a trap."

"But, I thought you said that it was James?" asked Joe.

"I am sure it is, but I want to prepare for the worst and hope for the best," said Steve.

The rest of the group was still in the dining area as Steve had asked.

"Men, let's go to the armory," said Steve. "Women and children to the lower level storage and take shotguns."

"What's happening?" asked Nancy.

"We think that men from Sanctuary Three are up top, but we want to be safe just in case they have unwelcome guests with them," said Joe.

The men went to the armory to put on body armor and side arms and to get more rubber shells for their shotguns. They all went back up, but Gary and Ray stayed below the bottom hatch and secured it behind Joe and Steve. Joe left his radio button pressed open with tape so that the others could hear everything that was going on as he and Steve opened the top hatch.

"Are you ready?" Steve asked Joe.

"Ready as I'll ever be."

With that, Steve opened the hatch and there was James, and Jake.

"Easy guys," said Jake. "Can you not point those things at us please?"

They lowered the shotguns and Steve crawled out with the Geiger counter. It said two Rads. "How long have you guys been exposed out here?" he asked.

"About four hours," said James. "We should be just fine."

"All the same, why don't both of you get in here so we can talk? We've had some unwanted visitors, and a balloon was shot down."

"That's why we're here," said Jake. "We had to kill these guys that were camped out here, they were acting crazy." He pointed to four bodies on the ground behind them.

"I'll get a camera to put up while we're inside, so we know it's safe to come back out," said Steve. He and the others went inside. Steve went back up with Joe to set the camera to rotate 360 degrees around the top hatch.

The scene in the common area was like a family reunion. Everyone knew James and Jake, and to see outsiders that they hadn't seen in almost a year was emotional, to say the least. James and Jake couldn't believe how big Karen was and asked when she was due. "Anytime now," she said with a big smile on her face.

"The news of your pregnancy will lift everyone's spirits," said James.

"What do you mean?" asked Karen.

"I'll fill you in later," said James. Steve had questions, and the others wanted to debrief them but they waited until the excitement died down.

"I know everyone is very excited to see these guys," said Steve. "But we really need to talk. Can we have the room for a while and I promise, you will not be kept in the dark." The women and kids left the common area so the men could talk.

"Okay guys, let us know all that you do," said Gary.

"Where to start?" asked James. "Well we were having issues with balloons and getting data. The last readings we got last month were around ten Rads, so we decided to open the hatch and send one up manually after the tube got plugged. We went prepared, but not prepared enough. As soon as we opened up, the shooting started. Two of our people, Matt and Mike, were shot and eventually succumbed to their wounds. The rest of us were able to fight off the attackers and drive them back. The levels were about four Rads at that point. We spent as little time as possible outside, but had to establish a perimeter. Once we put up a few cameras and motion sensors, we were able to defend the bunker more easily. When the sensors would go off, we would open up the hatch and take care of the threat. We wanted to get to you and Sanctuary Two, but being down two men already we didn't want to take the chance."

"Then why did you decide to come here now?" asked Gary.

"Two days ago we saw three figures coming toward the hatch just before dark. We went out to engage them and a firefight started outside before we got there. The three figures were Bill, Trevor and Susan. They were the only survivors of Sanctuary Two. They had to fight their way to us. With more people to protect our bunker, we made the decision to try to make it here. The marauders had done the same thing to all three bunkers by filling up the launch tubes with rocks and getting us to open up, but it turns out that you were the only smart ones."

"Don't say that," said Steve. "We all did what we thought was right and this is how things turned out. I'm just glad that you and the people that made it are still with us. We need to band together and survive. The equipment bunker is right behind yours, so it would make sense to hold up there with everyone we have left and make a well protected perimeter. How many more people are out there to threaten us, do you know?"

"We have killed a total of ten people," said James. "And I have no idea how many more are out there. We know they are hungry and pretty resourceful for being out in the radiation for almost a year. We don't know who any of them are."

"We have all been sending up balloons," said Steve. "They would be able to see them for many miles in this wasteland. We basically called them to us without knowing it."

"Were they able to get into the armory in Sanctuary Two?" asked Joe.

"We don't know," said Jake, "because we couldn't get close enough."

"Couldn't get close enough?"

"We came under fire as soon as we got within one hundred yards, so we made our way here instead."

"We need to get in there and see what's left," said Joe.

"That will have to be a priority," said James. "We need all the supplies we can get."

"How did Sanctuary Two get ambushed?" asked Gary.

"From what Trevor could tell us, they did what we all did and opened up their hatch. They unfortunately were not prepared for people to attack them either. By the time anyone got to the armory, most of the group had been killed. Bill and Trevor drove the marauders back up to the surface, but too many systems had been damaged to continue to stay in there, and who could blame them anyway with the carnage that was left inside. They took all the supplies they could and made their way to us," said James.

"What did you tell the others in your bunker?" asked Steve. "Are you supposed to be back by a certain time?"

"We told them that we would be back within twenty-four hours or not at all."

"Well, you will be back," said Joe, "and we will deal with this threat with decisive force."

"Alright," said Steve. "We'll make room for you tonight and we will go with you in the morning. Safety in numbers makes the most sense. We will figure out the best way to defend Sanctuary Three and the equipment bunker." The two men were set up in the common area with cots to sleep on. They were given a change of clothes and took showers to wash off any radiation particles still on them. It was pretty safe outside now, but precautions were still a good idea.

The next morning the men would go to Sanctuary Two on their way to Sanctuary Three and find out if anything was still usable inside, and if anyone was occupying it.

Sanctuary Three was almost two miles away, and with an unknown number of marauders out there, they were taking no chances. Joe recommended that they wear full combat gear. "It will slow us down a little," he said, "but will protect us better if we run into an ambush."

Everyone tried to get some sleep, but no one could stop thinking about the friends they had lost after surviving for eight months after the world ended. The only thing to do was to stick with the plan and rebuild. No one wanted to hurt anyone outside because they were just trying to survive as well, but their group had to be put first.

Chapter Thirteen: On the Move

The next morning it was very quiet around the table. The kids were told that it was still unsafe outside, but they had to go help the other sanctuary and wouldn't be gone long. "Short term exposure to the amount of radiation that is on the surface still shouldn't cause health issues," said Gary. "But you will want to take your potassium iodide pills just in case. You will want to wear your SCBA masks all the way if you can to avoid breathing in any particles, and use the Geiger counters all the way."

"You do know that we will more than likely be shooting at people and being shot at, right?" asked Joe.

"Yes, I know this," said Gary, "but this is the best advice I can give you from a medical standpoint. Oh, and don't get shot either."

"Thanks for the heads up," said Joe.

The men from Sanctuary One said their good-byes to their loved ones and put on their gear. Karen of course didn't want Steve to go, being so close to giving birth, but he assured her that he would be back before the baby came. Gary was the only man left back and for good reason. Karen was about to give birth and if anyone needed medical attention he would be ready to give it. They couldn't afford to lose one of their doctors.

They scanned the area with the camera set up on the surface, and Steve gave the all clear. The men opened the hatch and made their way out. Gary secured the hatch behind them and they were off to Sanctuary Two. They kept in contact with throat mics and radios on their backs. The push to talk button was attached to their gloves for convenience. This allowed them to hold their weapons at all times and still talk.

The plan was for two of them to move straight in on the bunker and the other three men would flank it from the same side. With very little cover, they were exposed all the way in. If they came under fire, they would throw smoke grenades upwind to mask their movement. With the supplied air tanks and masks, they would be able to smoke out the marauders if they were in the bunker too.

After walking for about an hour in the bright sunlight, the bunker was finally in sight. There was just a small amount of snow on the ground, but it seemed colder than it should be that time of year. The men split up to execute their plan. Jake and Ray moved toward the bunker from the front and got within fifty yards before people started to come out shooting.

"Contact front!" Yelled Jake on the radio as the firefight began.

Joe had split off for higher ground and started to cover Jake and Ray with sniper fire. This was not part of the plan, but was working out very well to their advantage.

Jake threw smoke grenades out in front of them and he and Ray took cover behind a small hill while Joe took the new enemy out. Joe didn't like what he was doing, but knew their very survival depended on it, and these people had killed his friends. It was payback time.

Joe counted seven people he had shot and radioed for Jake and Ray to move forward. Steve and James moved in as well. Joe would stay out and cover them just in case they were attacked while inside the bunker. The men surrounded the hatch and shined their weapon lights down. The lower hatch was closed which meant that someone was more than likely in there. The men they had killed on the surface were moved away and their weapons were piled up nearby.

Little did the marauders down in the bunker know, the contractor that built the hatches installed a safety lever on the outside so they could still be opened if they were locked from the inside.

The men got ready to drop smoke inside and wait for anyone to come out. They had shotguns with rubber slugs ready to use. It was decided that they needed answers from these people, about the number of people they had and any news on the world they left behind.

Steve opened the hatch just enough for Ray to drop two smoke grenades in. They all stood back and waited for people to come out. Within a few minutes, a woman, a man and two kids came out choking on the smoke. James and Jake pushed them up the ladder to the surface and told them to get on the ground. Steve and Ray joined them and put flexi cuffs on all the people, kids included.

"Is there anyone else inside?" asked Ray. They said nothing. "Once again, is there anyone else down there?" This time Ray shot a round into the dirt in front of them.

"No, we are all that is left," said the woman.

"Joe, you stay there and keep an eye on the area," said Steve over the radio. "And watch your back. We are going into the bunker."

"Be careful," said Joe. "I don't like this."

"We'll leave James here to guard these four and we will be right back."

The other three men slowly made their way down into the bunker with Jake leading the way. Jake was Sanctuary Three's gun guru since he had been in the Army. They made their way down each level, clearing each room as they did. The whole bunker was a mess, with trash everywhere and bloodstains from the original inhabitants more than likely. The men stayed together the whole way. After they were convinced that it was clear of more people, they made their way back up to tell the others.

Suddenly, a man came out of one of the closets on the first level behind the three men and stabbed Steve in the back. Ray turned around and opened fire with his AK-47, killing the man.

"Steve, are you ok?" asked Jake.

"I don't think he got me," said Steve.

"Turn around and let me look, said Jake.

Steve had so much gear and body armor on that the knife didn't make it through to his body.

"You're one lucky dude," said Jake.

They got to the surface and radioed for Joe to come down. He said he would stay up there until they were done. Steve stayed on top this time to watch the people and the other three went back down.

"I thought you were the last ones?" asked Steve.

"We thought we were," said the man.

"The armory door was shut," said Jake. "So they might not have gotten in."

"What about the food stores?" asked James.

"They looked pretty well gone through, but we might be able to salvage some."

The men made their way to the armory. The door had been beat to hell from them trying to get in. James hit the secret lever on the door and it opened. The contents of the armory were completely intact.

"Well that question has been answered," said Jake. "Now how do we get all of this out of here?"

"We have to leave it," said James. "It would take a truck to move it all and we're not bringing those out yet."

"So we just lock it up and hope they don't find the lever to open it?"

"Unfortunately yes," said James. "We will have to lock both top hatches and hope they can't get back in. We will come back when we can to salvage everything we can't carry out now." They locked the armory back up after taking some essentials and went down to the food storage room.

"What we can salvage in here, we can lock up in the armory too," said Ray.

"Good idea," said James. "We can go through the entire bunker and do that just in case they get back in here."

Jake went back up to the surface to let the other two know what they were doing. The weather had turned from clear to overcast and it was starting to snow.

"What should we do with these people?" asked Steve.

"We should kill them," said Joe over the radio.

"We can't do that, it's not right."

"It wasn't right for them to kill our friends or attack all three bunkers either."

"I wouldn't feel right about doing that," said Steve, "we're not those kinds of people."

"Yeah well not yet," said Joe. "Just wait until we *are* like them and see how you feel. Let them go then."

"We will make the decision as a group once the others get back up here."

"You better tell them to hurry," said Joe. Because it's getting cold out here."

"Jake can you tell them to hurry please?" asked Steve.

"On my way," said Jake as he went back down into the bunker.

"How are we doing down here guys?" asked Jake.

"Almost done," said Ray.

"It's starting to snow up there and we still need to get to Sanctuary Three."

"They have either destroyed the rest, or it has been used," said James. The men locked the armory door again and went back up to the surface.

"What are we going to do with them?" asked Steve.

"Have you gotten any information out of them?" asked James.

"They say that they are the only ones left and that they came here as they were walking south to a warmer climate. They saw our balloons and stopped to try to contact us. Some of the people in their group of around thirty were really sick and they needed help. They shot down the balloons in an attempt to get our attention, but it didn't work. So they filled up the tubes and waited. Some of the people started to get desperate and when the hatches opened they started shooting instead of being civil. They say because their kids are with them, they would not do this to us. They just want to survive," said Steve.

"Please help us," said the woman. The kids were crying.

"We don't know them and don't know if they are a threat," said Jake. "They could be the ones that started all of this and killed our friends."

"Do you have any identification on you?" asked James.

"No we don't," said the woman. "I am Sally Reynolds and this is my husband Kyle and our kids Allie and Trent. Please help us, the only reason we were with the others is because we knew we would be safer with more people. We just want to live."

"Blindfold them and bring them with us," said Steve. "Joe, it's time to go. How does the area look?"

"Not a movement anywhere for miles," he said.

Joe walked down to meet the others and they all started the walk to Sanctuary Three.

Chapter Fourteen: Home Sweet Home

"How will we contact the bunker in the dark?" Steve asked James as they approached it.

"I worked out a signal before we left. Everyone stop," said James.

He pointed his AK-47 towards the bunker and started to flash his weapon light. He told the sanctuary in Morse code, through the cameras, that he was home and he had brought some friends.

The hatch opened up and the area lit up with the light coming out of it. "Are you sure we should all go down?" asked Steve. "Will you have enough air?"

"We turned on our air supply from the surface when the radiation dropped to three Rads," said James. "The filters will handle it, and we needed more with the introduction of more people from Sanctuary Two."

"We can still go back tonight."

"Nonsense," said James. "You will be our guests tonight, now get in there."

"What about the prisoners?" asked Jake.

"They will be welcomed into our home as our new friends as long as they can be trusted," said James.

The outside temperature had dipped down to fifteen degrees and the snow continued to fall as they made their way into the bunker.

The outsiders were brought in front of the occupants of Sanctuary Three in the common area. Their flexi cuffs and their blindfolds were taken off.

"Where are we?" asked the girl, Allie.

"We are in our home," said James, "and you are welcome to stay."

"Really mommy?" asked Trent.

"Not that we don't want to be here or to sound ungrateful," said Kyle, "but why would you offer this to us?"

"We have all lost so much and we need to stop fighting and start rebuilding," said Steve. "If you can be trusted, we would like for you to stay. The three bunkers that we built before the end were for us to survive in and begin again. What kind of people would we be if we left you out in the cold and dying world?" asked James.

"We have rules for you to follow of course," said Jake.

"This will not be a free ride," said Trevor. "You will have to help out around here in order to be a part of our community. We do not plan on staying here long term, but we will as long as we need to."

"We will clear out a storage room and put cots in there for the time being," said Theresa, Mike's wife.

Olivia, one of the six children living in Sanctuary Three, was fourteen and growing up fast. She was very happy to see another teenage girl. The other children were all younger and annoying, according to Olivia.

"Would you like to see if some of my clothes fit you?" she asked Allie. "I can get you and your brother some tooth brushes and towels out of storage for your showers, too."

Allie couldn't believe it. It had been many months since she had brushed her teeth. "I really get to take a shower?" she asked Olivia.

Laughing, Olivia said yes. "We get to take one every four days." The two girls were instantly friends.

"Trevor and Susan are more than welcome to come back with us," said Steve, "And Bill if he wants. Where is he anyway?"

"He is working through losing his wife," said James. "He can stay here for now."

All the people that had just come in from outside needed to take off their gear and clothes and take showers, to get rid of radiation particles. This would take a while with nine of them. Some of the others started making room for all of the guests.

"Do you think we will have any more issues with people wanting in this winter?" Steve asked James.

"I don't think we will. Why don't we plan on staying down here until spring when it warms up, and then consolidate our forces and supplies?"

"Sounds like a great plan," said Steve.

Everyone took showers, ate dinner and got settled for the night. The new people couldn't believe all that was offered down in the bunker. They ate like they had never ate before and the kids acted like they had never watched TV. They knew that they had a good thing going with the bunker people and continually thanked everyone that night for the food, water and shelter.

They were told that they would go through an informal evaluation the next day to determine their spot in the community and how well they could contribute. A camera was put up in the hall just outside their room so they could be monitored for a while until they could be completely trusted.

The next morning, everyone showed up for breakfast and because of so many people needing to eat, two groups had to be served.

"We are making breakfast as quick as we can guys," said Theresa.

"We're in no hurry," said James. "We have no place to be."

A few people chuckled at what he said, because he was kind of joking about being stuck underground and all.

The group from Sanctuary One and Trevor and Susan ate in the first group, because they had to get back before too much more snow fell.

Steve and James decided to put up antennas with cables running down through the launch tubes, after they were cleaned out of debris, so they could stay in contact with each other until springtime. With no more need to launch balloons because of the current radiation levels continuing to drop, and not wanting to attract any more attention, the tubes would come in handy for communication. The antennas didn't have to be too big, with the short distance and nothing in the way of sight anymore. They couldn't be seen from a long distance this way either.

The group from Sanctuary One was all geared up and ready to go when Kyle and Sally walked up to them and thanked them for what they had done, and said how sorry they were they had lost their friends.

"We all have lost so very much," said Steve. "We need to cherish who we have left in our lives. The others and I would not have allowed you to stay here if we hadn't seen something good about you and your family. Just don't make us regret our decision."

"We won't," said Kyle and Sally, almost at the same time. Sally hugged the men and they started walking upstairs to leave.

"We should have our antenna and communication equipment up and running by tomorrow night," Steve said to James.

"We'll get ours put up right away," said James.

"See you soon brother," Joe said to Jake. "You get these people ready for anything we might encounter next year."

"I will," said Jake.

The two men had discussed tactics during Joe's brief stay and Jake liked the idea of the classes that Joe had been teaching in Sanctuary One to familiarize everyone with all of the weapons stored in the armory.

The three men from Sanctuary One left for their home on a cold and snowy morning with their new roommates. The trek back was even slower because of the snow that kept coming down, getting deeper by the minute. Luckily no resistance was encountered on the way back.

It took most of the day to get back, and a very tired Steve started to tap on the hatch with Morse code as soon as they arrived. Within a few minutes, Gary was opening the top hatch to let them in. Gary couldn't believe how much snow had fallen in the last day, as he looked around before closing the hatch.

The last Geiger counter reading was only registering trace amounts of radiation. The travelers got inside and took all of their gear off. They took showers and the heat was turned up for them. The others had questions, and were very happy to see Trevor and Susan.

Nancy organized the women to make room for their friends in one of the storage rooms. "We will make you as comfortable as we can," she told Susan. "I can't imagine what you have gone through. We are all here for you."

"Thank you," she told Nancy. Everyone was tired, and made an early night of it.

Early the next morning, Steve was already up and working on getting the air flowing from the surface through the NBC filters. He was also getting everything ready for the communication system to be put into place so they could stay in contact with Sanctuary Three.

Karen walked into the storage room, right beside the mechanical room. Steve had turned it into the communications room. "Are you ok honey?" Karen asked him.

"I'm doing great! I just want to get all of this ready to go so we can talk to the other bunker and make a plan to get out of here in the spring."

"Why can't we just stay here?" she asked.

"We can for a few more years, but we will eventually run out of supplies and I don't think we could survive in this climate."

"This climate?" Karen asked.

"Things have changed outside and I don't know why. It could be because of the radiation or all of the huge explosions, but we are defiantly having a major climate change. We got over three feet of snow in the first twenty-four hours this winter and it's still falling. We will have to get to a warmer climate and soon if we want to grow crops and survive."

Karen couldn't believe what she was hearing. "We just had our world destroyed and now we have to leave this place that has kept us all safe?" she asked. "What about our baby?"

"Things will not be easy," said Steve, "but we need to leave here just as soon as the weather will let us. We will be ok," he reassured her.

"So, tell me what exactly you are doing down here," she said.

"I turned on the air flowing from the surface," said Steve, "and now I am setting up a communications tower so we can talk to Sanctuary Three, and monitor the surface conditions with the sensors."

"Is it safe to be breathing the air from up there?" Karen was constantly worrying about the baby.

"We have filters and we could have turned it on months ago," said Steve. "You two will be just fine."

"I feel so bad about our friends that we lost," said Karen as she started to cry.

Steve knew it was hormones and hugged her again.

"Why don't you go see if anyone needs help? It will keep your mind occupied. I will be up to see you just as soon as I get all of this up and running." Karen relented and left.

Gary came into the room and asked how long he had been up.

"I couldn't really sleep," said Steve. "You here to help?" he asked Gary.

"Tell me what you need."

The two men finished up putting the system together. "Now we need to go up to set up the antenna and drop the cable down to hook into this," said Steve.

"Who will go up to the surface?" asked Gary.

"I will," said Joe. He was dressed in cold weather gear and had his mask in his hand. "Just tell me what to do guys."

They all went up stairs to the surface to get everything in place. Jake opened up the bottom hatch with some trouble. It was slightly frozen.

"This isn't a good sign," said Steve. "I put sensors on the antenna that I took off the balloons so we could get temperature and Rad readings, so let's just get this done and we can get all the information we need."

The top hatch took all three men to open. It was frozen too and had a lot of snow on it. "How could this have happened in just a day?" yelled Gary. It was a blizzard out there. Joe was to attach the antenna to what was left of the cabin and drop the cable down through the launch tube.

It took him longer than was expected to attach the antenna, and it was getting cold. He had to uncover the launch tube in order to drop the cable. As soon as he dropped the cable down, he attached it to the antenna and was ready to go back down.

He was frozen by the time he got back in and the hatches were closed. "It's got to be subzero out there," he said as the other two helped him get his gear off.

"We will know just as soon as I get the cable hooked into the computer," said Steve.

"Thanks for doing that," said Gary, as he looked at Joe's fingers and toes for frostbite. "Get warm and take a shower. Come down and see us when you're done."

Joe left and Gary followed Steve downstairs. "What do you think?" he asked Steve as he walked into the room.

"I don't like the looks of things up there."

"I'm glad I'm not the only one," said Gary. "Something strange is happening."

"I agree," said Steve. "And we need to figure it out. We are experiencing a climate change, but is it localized or global?"

Steve pulled the cable out of the launch tube and pushed the snow out of the way. A few minutes later he had it hooked up and was ready to switch it all on.

Joe walked in and Gary said, "Perfect timing! You can see what your hard work has allowed us to see." Steve turned it on and data began to show up.

"It's thirty-eight below zero!" exclaimed Steve. "The wind is blowing twenty-five miles an hour and gusts are reaching forty."

"No wonder I was cold out there," said Joe.

"Try the radio," said Gary. "Sanctuary Three, this is Sanctuary One, can you hear me?" asked Steve. They heard nothing, so Steve tried again.

"This is Sanctuary Three," James finally answered.

"What's the weather like over there?" asked Steve.

"The worst I have ever seen it," said James.

"Same here," said Steve. "Do you have any ideas about why it's so bad?"

"Well," said James. "We are definitely experiencing a climate change, but why?"

"I agree," said Steve. "A polar shift maybe?"

"Could be, we should just keep an eye on it."

"Will do, how are the new underground citizens doing?"

"They're fitting in just fine. How is Bill?"

"He hasn't said too much lately," said James.

"I hope he makes it through this," said Steve.

"That goes for all of us. Keep in touch," said James. "I'm going to recommend contact every twelve hours from this time unless more is warranted."

"Sounds like a plan," said Steve.

The radio was left running just in case contact was initiated. Steve was leaving the communication room when Kim came running toward him and said that Gary needed him in the medical room right away. Steve went up as fast as he could and heard screaming as he entered the room. There was blood on the floor and Gary was calling for more help restraining Karen.

"What is happening?" Steve asked, very concerned.

"She is hemorrhaging from placenta previa more than likely," said Gary. "We will have to perform an emergency c-section. When did her water break?" Gary looked at Steve.

"I didn't know it had. Please save her," said Steve.

"I will do everything I can," said Gary. "Please have Joe, Nancy and Ray stand by to give blood. Trevor will start getting it from them as soon as he is done assisting me. Karen will need as much as we can give her," said Gary.

Karen was given local anesthetics to get her ready for the c-section, and Gary performed the procedure as fast and as carefully as possible. Karen's blood pressure was dropping when the baby came out. He was just fine and Gary put him in a basket with a lamp above him to keep him warm. Then all focus went back to Karen and to the people that were giving blood at that point. Gary with Nancy assisting him sewed Karen up while Trevor took blood from the donors.

Karen soon stabilized, but everyone stayed for a few more hours just in case she needed more blood. Steve thanked everyone for their help, especially Gary and Trevor. "What's his name Steve?" asked Nancy.

"De Novo," said Steve.

"Day what?" asked Nancy.

"It's Latin for, 'from the beginning,' or 'new,'" said Steve. "I think it's appropriate for his name considering he is our new beginning."

"I agree," said Nancy. "I like it. Do you think Karen will also?"

"I think that Karen will like it for many reasons," said Steve.

"I'm going to go tell everyone," said Nancy as she quickly and excitedly walked away.

Chapter Fifteen: New Situations

The people in Sanctuary Three were very interested to hear everything Sally and Kyle knew and had seen.

"Where did you come from?" asked Kerri, Jake's wife.

"We made our way here from Great Falls," said Sally. "We met more people on the way who were heading south. Most of the people were good and wanted to help the group, but things started to get more desperate by the day as more people joined us and the little bit of supplies we had disappeared. Things got bad."

"What do you mean?" asked Theresa.

"Well," began Sally, "people started to vanish with no explanation. A few people had guns and just started to take what they wanted. One day, some of the people saw a balloon floating up in the air and that's how your bunkers were found. The people with the guns were ready to just get in and take what they wanted. Kyle, me and a few others wanted to talk to you, but the others said the days for talking were long gone and it was every man for himself. I am so sorry that this all happened to you nice people. We only took shelter in the bunker they took, for the children's sake. We wanted to meet the people in the bunker, not hurt them," said Sally.

"That is the past," said Sherri. "Now we are all in this together. Sally, I need to know what your occupation used to be."

"I was a school teacher," she said.

"Great, you can help Debbie out with the school she set up for the kids. Kyle, what did you do?"

"I was a heavy equipment mechanic for a mining company."

"Great, we will fit you in somewhere. As well as your areas of expertise, we all share in the everyday duties and there is a rotation schedule for this. You will be added in for the next rotation and we expect you might not like what you have to do from time to time, but what we offer is better than anything on the surface. We are all glad we are here even when we are scrubbing toilets," Sherri said with a smile.

"Do any of you have any questions?"

"Not at this time," said Kyle, "but if we do later do we talk to you?"

"Yes, I have been given the title of host and problem solver. I used to be a corporate administrator and it has come in pretty handy down here."

"Please don't hesitate to ask anyone if you have questions though. I have put together a small list of guidelines that the rest of us already adhere to. I hope you can live with them. It was very nice talking with you both," said Sherri. "See you around."

"Doesn't she know that we will see each other all the time?" Kyle asked Sally.

"Be nice, you don't want to be on the surface again, and the kids will be so much better off here."

"I know you're right," said Kyle, "but I am still pissed off at myself for not helping their friends."

"If you had, you might not be here either," said Sally.

"How are they doing?" James asked Sherri as she walked into the new communications room.

"I think they will fit in just fine. I might have a problem with them if they didn't have kids. They have more to lose having them and will cooperate better I think."

"You might be right about that."

"Did you get a hold of Sanctuary One yet?"

"I just talked to Steve a little while ago," said James.

"How are they doing?"

"Well, Steve had the bright idea to attach sensors from one of the balloons to the communications antenna, so we have temperature and radiation readings."

"How bad is it honey?"

"It's thirty-eight below zero, strong winds and over four feet of snow."

"My god, and the radiation levels?" asked Sherri.

"They are virtually gone," said James.

"What does this bad weather mean?"

"Steve and I agree that the earth has undergone or is still undergoing a climate change. We will need to get to a warmer climate in order to grow crops and find wild game. We can only survive here for a little longer," said James. "Oh and Karen had her baby too."

"You waited that whole time to tell me?" Sherri asked as she hit James on the arm.

"I was saving the best for last," he said with a smile.

"Well, is it a boy or a girl and what did they name the little miracle?" asked Sherri.

"She had a boy and they named him De Novo."

"Ok," said Sherri. "You will have to explain that one to me. What does it mean and where did Steve come up with it?"

"Steve said it's Latin for, 'from the beginning,' or 'new,'" said James. "He thought it was a great and appropriate choice for the world we now live in."

"I agree," said Sherri. "I will have to go and tell everyone," she quickly left the room.

Steve was just about to check in with James again the next day when James called first. "Hello Sanctuary One is anyone there?"

"I am here James, go ahead."

"You have anything new or out of the ordinary over there?" asked James. "It's all pretty much the same," said Steve. "How are your new people doing?"

"So far so good," said James.

"I don't think they want to ruin a good thing," said Steve.

"I think you're right. How are Karen and the baby doing?" asked James.

"The baby is doing great and Karen is looking much better, thanks for asking."

"You bet," said James. "Let's just keep in contact and hopefully we don't have any more excitement for a while."

Christmas wasn't the same for anyone, but the women in both sanctuaries tried to make the best of the situation. Dinner was the same as usual, but they decorated and did their best.

No one really wanted to celebrate New Year's. Things were different now and no one felt in the mood.

One afternoon in January an alarm sounded and everyone met in the common area. "That's the hatch right?" asked Joe.

"Unfortunately," said Steve.

Joe took charge all of a sudden. "Steve, get on the radio and inform Sanctuary Three, all women and children to the lower level. The rest of you men, follow me to the armory." No one missed a beat and went in different directions.

"Ray, take this radio down to Steve please. Can you have him turn the alarm off and come right back? All nonlethal guys," said Joe.

They put on tactical vests and loaded shotguns with rubber slugs. Ray came back up and initiated a radio check. They heard a good to go from everyone.

The men slowly made their way to the bottom hatch. "Ready?" asked Joe. "Open it up." Ray and Trevor opened the hatch and pointed their weapons up with lights on. "They haven't made it past the top hatch," Joe said over the radio for everyone to hear.

"Opening the top hatch now," said Joe. It took three of them to open the frozen door. They lit up the immediate area around the bunker with their weapon lights and saw two bodies in the snow.

"Who are they?" asked Ray.

"It's Craig and Simon. Get them in here," said Steve.

They were very cold and Simon wasn't breathing. Steve got on the radio and said, "Gary, we have an emergency. Get Trevor and...."

"Coming to you," said Gary.

Ray secured the hatches and went down to meet them. "What the hell are they doing here?" asked Gary as they carried them to the medical room. "I thought you said they had been killed Trevor?"

"It was crazy that day and we couldn't find them after it was all over. Where have they been?"

"Let's worry about that later," said Gary. "Right now they are in real trouble with hypothermia and frostbite. Everyone else get out please."

"Good job Joe," said Steve afterward.

"I didn't mean to, the words just came out."

"It needed to be done, everyone listened to you and we are all safe. Go secure the armory and get everyone settled down."

Steve went back to the radio to inform James of the situation. "Are they going to make it?" he asked.

"We won't know until Gary and Trevor get done with them. I will let you know just as soon as I know," said Steve.

Steve went back to the medical room to wait for any word. Gary walked out almost an hour later. A few others had joined Steve in the hall.

"Did they make it?" asked Steve.

"They are both stable, but we might have to amputate some parts. We won't know for a while."

"Are they awake? Did they tell you anything?"

"No, they didn't speak and are both asleep. We will take turns watching them until they are out of the woods," said Gary.

Everyone left and went about their night. "What do you think happened to them Steve?" asked Karen.

"I can only guess that they went out after the marauders when they were attacked and have either been lost or in captivity," said Steve. "Where could they have been is best question. As far as I know there is nowhere to stay out of the weather other than our bunkers. We will all know soon enough, though," said Steve.

The two men were in and out of consciousness for days. Craig was the first one to wake up and start to talk.

It was as Steve had thought. In the confusion of the attack on Sanctuary Two, Craig and Simon had gone up after the marauders and were captured after putting up a hell of a fight. There was a cave a few miles away that they had been staying in. It was a shit hole according to Craig, but it was a place to stay out of the elements. The two dozen or so men and women were blowing through the supplies they had scavenged out of the bunker. Bill and Trevor had done well getting them out, but they had taken a lot before being driven off.

"They were animals and I for one am surprised they kept us alive as long as they did," Craig told everyone in the room. "We witnessed beatings and rapes of women and some of the kids. I wanted to kill them all, but I couldn't get out of my bindings. Things were bad, but got worse after the snow started to fall.

Simon and I had been tortured for information on getting into the other bunkers. We told them that we only knew how to get into ours. After seeing them result to cannibalism, we knew our days were numbered. We had to get out of there and fast," he said. "We were given just enough water to stay alive."

"One of the women had lost her husband when the bombs fell and survived by doing whatever the leaders of the pack wanted. She saw us as her way out and untied us one night."

"On our way out of the cave, one of the men woke up and started yelling. The woman was right behind us, but I don't think she even made it out. We just kept going, and this was the closest friendly place."

"Ok Craig," said Gary. "Why don't you rest for a while?"

"Get me better brother. As soon as I can I am going back out there and killing them all and God can sort them out." Gary closed the curtain around the bed and motioned for Steve to follow him.

"Craig has lost two toes and part of a finger, he had more and heavier clothes on than Simon" said Gary.

"What about Simon?" asked Steve.

"He is really bad off and I have removed more than I care to say."

"Will he make it?"

"I don't know at this point," said Gary. "I will let you know what happens as time goes by. You should probably warn Joe that Craig might want into the armory," said Gary.

"I will do that right now."

The days passed and Craig got better, and Simon started talking. Everyone heard what the two men had gone through and were ready to help them when they needed it.

Joe walked by the armory one morning and heard yelling. He walked in to see Craig trying to get into it.

"Can I help you buddy?" asked Joe.

"Let me in, I need to get in," said Craig.

"I don't think that's such a good idea right now man," said Joe.

"I need to get back out there and finish what I started," said Craig.

"Craig, as soon as the weather breaks, I will walk point for you and take them out with you. But until the snow melts you should stay here. You almost died getting out of there and need to get better."

"Don't tell me what I need; you have no idea what I need!" said Craig.

"I don't know your story, but I am willing to listen and help in any way I can," said Joe.

Gary and Trevor walked into the room and talked Craig into going back to the medical room.

"I will be right here when you're ready man," Joe told Craig. Everyone left the room. Joe went to talk to Steve. "I think we need to have Craig talk to Bill."

"I don't know," said Steve.

"I think it will help the both of them," said Joe. "Craig is ready to go and kick some ass and Bill won't even leave his room."

"I will talk to James and get his opinion."

"Thanks," said Joe.

Chapter Sixteen: New Beginnings

James knocked on the door and asked Bill if he could come in. Bill said nothing, so James walked in. "Bill, can I talk to you?"

"What do you want?"

"I just got off the radio with Steve in Sanctuary One and they had some visitors show up over there recently."

Bill walked out of the shadows and asked, "Who?"

"Craig and Simon showed up on their doorstep the other day."

"I don't believe you, why are you doing this?" asked Bill.

"It's true and Craig would like to talk to you. Come with me to the communication room," said James. Bill walked slowly behind him and as they walked downstairs. Everyone said hi to Bill, but he said nothing back.

Theresa and Debbie had lost their husbands when they were attacked and could sympathize with him, but they had their kids to help them through it, and he had no one really. Everyone was there for him, but somehow it wasn't enough. They all knew each other before everything went to hell, so it helped.

James and Bill reached the lower level communication room and sat down to call Sanctuary One.

"Hello Steve, are you there?" asked Jim.

"Go ahead," said Steve.

"I have Bill here, is Craig with you?"

"Hey Bill, its Craig man, how are you holding up?"

"I didn't believe them when they said you and Simon were still alive."

"We made it, but just barely."

"I am so sorry I let you guys down in there Craig. I should have done more."

"You did all that anyone could have done buddy. I am sorry about Elaine, if only we had been more prepared," said Craig.

"We couldn't have known that they were just up there waiting. I'm glad you guys made it," said Bill. "I'm looking forward to seeing you when the snow melts."

"Same here," said Craig. "You just hang in there and we will get payback, I promise." The radio went silent and the two men, miles apart and deep underground, went back to their rooms already feeling the satisfaction for the future revenge that they knew they'd take.

Theresa was growing more and more concerned about Bill. She and Elaine had worked with each other at the college and of course their families had been good friends. She decided to go and see him and offer whatever comfort she could. Bill's door was open when she got there so she knocked and slowly walked in.

"Bill, are you here?" she asked.

"What can I do for you?"

"Bill, it's Theresa," she said.

"I know, your voice could be picked out of a crowd. How are you?" he asked as he turned on a light.

"I am doing as well as can be expected," she said. "Olivia is keeping me busy so I don't lose it. I'm here for you if you want to talk."

"That's very kind of you," said Bill. "I'm sorry that I have been so standoffish toward everyone."

"No, don't be. We understand that you are dealing with your loss in your own way. We all went into this knowing that it would be hard and things like this might happen. Would it have been better for it to end fast like it did for all of the other people?" asked Theresa. "Sometimes I think it would have, but then I think about Olivia and how she hasn't had a chance to live her life yet."

"Bill, we all need to come to terms with everything that has happened to us or it will just eat us up, and we will be of no use to the people that are still counting on us. Please come out and at least eat a meal with us and feel the warmth of the room. We miss your company and would love to see you." Theresa walked over, gave him a hug and left. There was an emotion that both of them felt, but wouldn't let each other bring to the surface, not now, it would be wrong. They had known each other for years, but they had both just lost their spouses and knew that anything they felt was probably a longing for their lost ones. Or was it?

"How did it go in there?" asked James, as Theresa walked down the hall.

"I think I got through to him," she said.

"We need him to be ok," said James.

"I think he will be with time."

"You coming to dinner?"asked James.

"I am going to find my daughter and we'll meet you there."

Everyone was eating the evening meal when Bill walked in.

"Over here," said Theresa. "Olivia and I saved you a seat." Bill said nothing, but walked over and sat down. Sherri got up and got him a plate. She brought it over to him and he thanked her with a nod.

The room started to fill with conversation and Bill looked more at ease. After dinner, Theresa asked Bill if he would like to join her and some of the others for a card game. He hesitated for a minute and then said, "I would love to."

Bill stayed up playing cards for hours and even smiled a little. He thanked everyone at the end of the night and walked back to his room. The next morning he was at breakfast and seemed to be happier. After he was done eating, Bill walked up to James and asked him if he had anything for him to do.

"As a matter of fact," said James, "the air supply system is past due for maintenance."

"I'll get right on it," said Bill. "Let me know if there's anything else, will you?"

"I sure will," said James. Both men went about their duties and things seemed to be getting back to normal.

The next scheduled check in between the bunkers went well, with James telling Steve about Bill's progress and Steve telling James about Craig and Simon. Craig was chomping at the bit to get out and exact his revenge on the marauders, but otherwise was healing just fine. Simon was up and walking now and healing too.

The sensors on the antenna were still working and radiation levels were within norms. The temperature was holding around freezing, jumping above from time to time. When springtime would arrive was unknown at this point because of the severe winter, but everyone was ready for it.

Craig was helping the rest of the group with their duties since he wasn't allowed in the armory for now. He was their keystone, and everyone was aware of it. He understood that the others didn't want to be put at risk and he knew that his friends would have his back when the time came.

Simon was up and doing things as well, but his frostbite injuries were more severe and he had lost more fingers and toes as well as the tip of his nose. But he was coping with all of it very well. Simon and Craig were some of the single people that had joined up with the group. This did make things easier for their recovery, but they had to be lonely. The rest of the group was doing their best to keep the two men's minds from wandering by involving them in work and activities.

Things had been exciting, interesting, sad and lonely in the bunkers for everyone at different times since the bombs fell and yet, life went on.

The classes that people took turns teaching allowed everyone to learn to help out more in areas that they would never have explored in the world that was left behind.

Steve called James on the radio one day in April and asked, "Has anyone been outside?"

James replied, "No, should we?"

"We're getting pretty warm readings," said Steve. "The outside temperature has been in the mid-forties. We should at least look outside and maybe put up a camera if it stays warm out." Both men agreed.

"I will be the one to open the hatch to do it," James said. Jake, James and Kyle went to the hatches to open them and see how things looked on the surface.

All standard precautions were put into place, but Kyle had no weapon and understood why. He knew he would have to prove himself to be trusted fully. Kyle opened the hatch as the other two stood ready with shotguns. As soon as the top hatch was opened up, water poured in and the other guys yelled, "Close it, close it now!" Kyle struggled, but got it closed.

"What the hell is going on?" yelled a soaked Jake.

"We are obviously in an area that has been flooded with all the melting snow," said James.

After the men dried off and the water had been cleaned up, James called Steve on the radio. "No good over here," said James. "We have shut off the air flow from the surface for now and gone back to relying on the plants."

"We'll take precautions and open our hatch in the morning," said Steve.

"Let us know if you get the same results," said James.

The next morning Steve, Joe and Ray got the whole house together in the common area and ready for evacuation if water flowed and the hatch couldn't be shut again. Ray opened the bottom hatch with the other two ready, then he opened the top hatch and no water came in, just bright sunlight.

"Go out slowly," said Steve. Ray went out, followed by Jake and then Steve. They could see that the small stream that cut through the valley had turned into a raging river because of the snow melting. They attached a camera to the antenna and the men went back down below.

Steve called James on the radio to give him the news. It was agreed that everyone would stay inside until the river level receded. The camera would be able to show them when that happened. After it went down, people from Sanctuary One would make their way to Sanctuary Three to make sure they could get out.

Two weeks went by and a select group was ready to leave and head over to Sanctuary Three. Steve, Joe, Ray and Craig would leave early on a sunny Saturday morning to go help their friends. Steve had pulled Craig aside to make sure his head would be in the game. Craig said he would wait until the group was ready before going to the cave to reconcile with the marauders. They left with enough weapons, gear and ammo to fight a small war. They had no idea what they might encounter, but they would be ready.

Chapter Seventeen : Dark Days

Craig was on point as soon as the men left the bunker. He insisted he was one hundred percent. They just let him do his thing and figured it would be for the best.

They encountered no resistance on the way to Sanctuary Three. Craig barked out orders and said, "Cover the flanks and give me a perimeter," when what was left of the cabin was in sight. They did what he asked and covered all sectors with overlapping fire.

There was water covering the ground where the hatch was. The water was receding and most of the snow in the immediate area had melted. It wouldn't be long before all the water would be gone and the hatch to the bunker could be opened. Steve tapped on the hatch in Morse code to let them know the situation.

"We should leave," said Ray, "and come back when the water is gone." It was agreed and the men left and went back to Sanctuary One.

On the way back Steve said, "We should wait a week and return." *It still isn't very warm out for the time of the year*, he thought.

They reached the bunker and waved in front of the camera for the hatches to be opened up. Gary met them at the opening and they all went inside.

"You didn't have any luck I take it?" asked Gary.

"The hatch was still covered with water," said Joe. "We will have to wait until the water level goes down."

"You didn't have any contact or see anyone else out there either?" asked Gary.

"Nothing out of the ordinary," said Steve. "Except it isn't very warm out."

"You're right," said Gary. "It should be warmer out by now."

"We'll see how things are next week when we go back out. In the meantime, we need to take a complete inventory of everything that we have," said Steve. All of the men went down below.

People went about their duties for the next week, but they couldn't wait to go back out and start life over again on the surface. Steve kept in contact with James and both bunkers had people working on getting a complete inventory of all water and supplies. There was excitement in the air in both bunkers. The thought of finally starting over was the main topic on everyone's lips.

The time came to go back out and hope that enough water was gone to open Sanctuary Three's hatch. The same group of men prepared to go back out. They geared up and Gary gave the all clear to open the hatch. The men were all out and were ready to leave when Craig started shooting then ran south along the river. Before anyone could stop him, he was out of sight.

"What the hell just happened?" asked Ray.

"I have only one guess," said Steve. "He saw one or more of the marauders and went after them."

"We need to help him," said Joe, as he started toward the same direction that Craig had gone.

"No, what we need to do is have Gary keep watch and get to Sanctuary Three as soon as we can. If Craig stirs up the hornets' nest, then we will need all the help we can get." They started for the bunker, hearing rifle fire ring out every once in a while.

The three men made record time to the bunker. There was still water on top of the hatch.

"We need to dam up some area upstream and reroute the water so we can get this open," said Steve. The three men took off their gear and started to take apart the cabin. They blocked an area fifty feet upstream of the hatch and kept adding to it. They took their camp shovels off their packs and started to shovel dirt up too. Ray started to bring in big rocks to help build it up. The dam turned into a dike that skirted the outside of the hatch. After a few hours of hard work, the water was no longer flowing over the bunker and with the warmth of the structure it had completely receded.

Steve tapped on the hatch and a few minutes later it opened up. Everyone, even the kids, started to come out. Steve took James aside and told him about Craig. James asked if everyone could go back down because the dike that was made to divert the water might not hold. "We will have plenty of time to come back up after we reinforce it," he told them. Joe stopped Jake and told him, "Get every able bodied man in full combat gear and enough supplies for a week per person, I'll explain when you all come back up." Jake did what he was asked and didn't question it.

When the others got back up with weapons and gear, Steve, Ray and Joe were ready again. "So what's going on?" Jake asked Joe. All of the men circled up and Steve explained the situation.

"We need to get Craig back," said Steve. Steve had an idea where the cave that Craig and Simon had been held might be so they all followed him. The men walked for miles and saw no one.

It was getting close to dark when the seven men arrived at the mouth of the cave. They decided to search it.

"We all go in together, and leave together," said Jake.

"Everyone put your silencers on your weapons," said Joe. "The last thing we need is to cause a cave in with the load noise of shooting. If we encounter resistance, fall back outside immediately."

"We will do what we came to do and leave for Sanctuary One as soon as we have Craig," said Steve. Everyone checked each other's weapons and gear. Jake was on point as they entered the cave. There was a horrible smell coming from inside.

Jake whispered on the radio, "It smells like death in here." They came out of a tunnel into a large room and the smell was even worse. Jake was motioning for the others to cover the flanks. As weapon lights filled the room, no one could believe the carnage that was laid out in front of them. Ray and James vomited. There were human heads on stakes and blood and entrails all over the place. "Do you think Craig did this?" asked Ray.

"I don't think he could do this," said Steve, "but if he did then we have a whole new problem."

Joe took charge as everyone reeled in shock. "I want teams of two to search this place and then we leave." Nothing new was found in the search, so they went back outside.

It was dark when they got out. "What kind of monsters could have done that?" asked James.

"None that we want to come in contact with," said Joe.

"Everyone get on their NVG's," said Jake. "We don't want to let anyone know we are out here by using lights that can be seen for miles."

The men left for Sanctuary One to stay there for the night. With still no sign of Craig, and after seeing the cave, everyone was on edge.

"Not a word of this to anyone," said Steve over the radio as they made their way back to the bunker.

"I think that's a great idea," said James, and everyone else agreed.

As it was dark when the men got back, they used a red light to flash Morse code into the camera for Gary to see. The hatch was opened up and they all climbed in. The men went to the commons and dropped their gear. Joe and Jake collected the weapons to be put in the armory. Cots were brought out of storage for the guys from Sanctuary Three. They all showered, ate and got ready for the next day. Steve and James got on the radio to let Sanctuary Three know what was going on and that they would be gone for at least another day in order to try to find Craig. Everyone tried to get some sleep, but no one really did.

A big breakfast was put together for the entire sanctuary. The women wanted the men to have a good meal before they left to go look for Craig. After breakfast, weapons were brought out of the armory and dispersed. Everyone said goodbye and made their way to the surface.

Jake and Joe discussed with everyone what they should do if they encountered any hostiles. "It would be nice if we had a plane or access to a satellite," said Ray. "I don't like the fact that we can't see where anyone might be hiding."

"I agree," said Steve, "but we will just have to be careful." They left for the area of the cave to look for Craig.

The sun was high in the sky but it was still pretty cold out when they reached the cave. Four of them would go in to check it one more time and the other three would cover the entrance. Ray wanted to get a better view, so he went up the mountain on top of the cave with his binoculars. He started scanning the area and saw some movement to the north. He radioed what he saw down to James and Bill. The other men had just come out of the cave with nothing more to report. Joe and Jake made their way up the mountain to where Ray was to get a better view.

"I can't make it out," said Ray. Jake got a spotting scope out of his pack and set it up. Once he got it focused he could see that it was a man crucified on a pole, more than likely a fence pole. Jake showed the others. "Should we go and check it out?" Ray asked.

"Yes we should," said Joe, and the men walked back down to meet up with the others.

"Could it be a trap?" asked James.

"I don't think so," said Joe. "There's no one else around for miles, at least from what I could see."

"Let's follow the bread crumbs," said Steve. They left and made their way toward the unknown man.

A small rise lay in front of them as they got closer. Jake called a halt to the group and everyone took a knee to listen to what he had to say. Jake told them to drop their packs and to break up into two groups. "I don't want to cause a crossfire here, so watch where the other group is at all times. If you lose sight of the other group on the flank, stop and break radio silence in order to find them again. No shooting unless shot at first and make damn sure that the person shooting is shooting at you and a real threat."

The two groups went separate ways around the rise and started crawling to the top. It was a lone man strung up on an old fence pole, and it wasn't Craig. The man was still alive, but barely. Steve and Ray cut him down while the others watched the area.

"Who are you?" asked Steve. The man couldn't talk and they soon found out why. His tongue had been cut out and his eyes and ears had been removed with something small and dull.

"Someone didn't like this guy," said Joe.

"What are we going to do with him?" asked James. "I don't think we should bring him back and let the others see how he has been treated."

"I agree," said Steve. "We should just leave him here and let his fate be sealed. We got him down and if he is to survive then it will be up to him."

"With no tongue to call for help, no eyes to see and no ears to hear, we are just going to leave this man here?" asked Joe.

"What do you expect us to do?" asked James. "Care for everyone we come across.

"Well it would be the right thing to do wouldn't it?"

"Maybe in the world we left behind," said Steve, "but this is a new one and we have to watch out for each other." Joe knew what they were saying was true, but he still had a problem with the humanity of things.

The man was left there for a reason and they didn't know why. So they did what they thought was right. They cut him down and left the rest up to him. It was better than just leaving him up there, most of them agreed.

They left with hopes of getting back before dark. Craig was still out there and they wanted to find him, but the security of the group had to be paramount. They made it back to Sanctuary One before dark and to stay for another night. They needed to get into the bunker in the side of the mountain in order to get more supplies out for building a perimeter around it and Sanctuary Three. The next day they would make their way back and try to get in, even though they didn't know if they would be able to.

Chapter Eighteen: No Surprise

The next day the same seven men left for Sanctuary Three and the bunker in the mountain. They met no resistance once again on their way and were glad. No one wanted a fight, but all were prepared just in case.

Once they reached Sanctuary Three that morning, they let them know what was going on and that they planned to try to enter the bunker to get out supplies and machinery to build the perimeter.

The men walked up to the big doors of the bunker that had been built into the side of the mountain strictly for extra supplies. "Do you know how to get in?" Steve asked James.

"I was hoping you knew," he said.

"This one was built by the same contractor right?" asked Joe.

"Yes it was," said Steve. The two men understood each other and looked for a release mechanism to open the door. Ray walked over to the right side and said, "I think I found it." He reached his hand into a hole and Joe grabbed him and pulled him back.

"Easy," said Joe, "let's get a light in there just to be certain it's not a Craig trap."

"I see a lever," said Joe. "Get me a stick or a pole." Ray gave him a stick and as it went in they heard a crunching sound. Joe pulled the stick out and saw that it had been cut off clean.

"That was almost your hand," Joe said to Ray.

"It's something else," said Ray, "we should keep looking."

The men searched for a few hours before Steve finally said, "I think...I think I found it." He was looking right at the two big doors at the opening. "It's right in front of us," he said. "Joe go and get your rifle." Steve took the rifle from Joe and said, "Stand back." Steve fired a round into a small hole in the door under some Latin words, which they soon found out meant, "Fire in the hole." The doors opened and everyone backed up.

The supply bunker was mainly put together by Craig and Don from Sanctuary Two. Some of the money for the supplies was put in by others, but the supplies were picked by Craig and Don.

No one really knew what was in the bunker until it was opened except Craig, and he was gone again. It was bigger than anyone had imagined. It had a huge tanker in the center with a Kenworth tractor hooked to it. It was full of diesel fuel. Four Humvees were lined up, more than likely purchased at a military auction. They had been up armored and had probably seen combat in the Middle East. Two more Kenworth tractors were attached to two forty-foot vans. The vans had been converted to be used as Mobil housing units with living quarters, bathrooms and entertainment areas.

In the back of the bunker, they found Conex boxes full of munitions and weapons from handguns to heavy machine guns, mortars and rockets. One crate was labeled, "Land mines and claymore mines." More Conex boxes were full of food.

"What were these guys planning to do?" asked James, who couldn't believe what he was seeing.

"Looks to me like they planned on surviving," said Jake.

Craig was the one that suggested building the supply bunker into the side of the mountain behind Sanctuary Three. He had been in the Marine Corps as a Special Forces Officer, the rank of Colonel. He was the gun guru of Sanctuary Two and believed dead until he showed up over the winter at Sanctuary One with Simon.

"Should we be going through all of this stuff?" asked Jake.

"Some of us helped pay for this stuff," said Steve, "so yes it's ok."

"Does anyone see a Bobcat anywhere?" asked Ray. "It's on this manifest I found at the entrance."

"It's over here," said Joe pointing.

"See if you can get it started," said Ray. "We will need it for the perimeter construction."

Joe and Jake were responsible for the designing and construction of the perimeter in conjunction with James and Steve as the engineers. It was to be a fortress that no one could get into. Land mines would be put out strategically around the entire perimeter as a first line of defense. The light and heavy machine guns were pulled off of the four Humvees for use in the towers that would be built. This would work great in the warmer weather, but if the snow fell like it did the previous winter then the newly built compound would be difficult to defend. But would it have to be? If the winter was that bad, then would anyone go out in it? It was a gamble, but one that might have to be considered.

Everyone from Sanctuary One was moved to Sanctuary Three, where they made room for the new inhabitants. Much of the supplies that weren't required for everyday living were moved to the supply bunker. The nights were cold so everyone slept in the bunker. The first part of construction would have to be walls to protect them. This would take some time as there was little left around the area for building material.

One day when a few men were trying to figure out what to use to build the walls, Billy walked up to them and asked about all the wood and other stuff from the other bunkers. The men stopped and looked at each other.

"Great thinking, I wonder whose kid this is," Ray said.

He tried to hug Billy, but the boy was too macho and said, "Get away old man." Everyone laughed and took the idea to the others.

The Hummers really helped getting all the materials from the other bunkers and construction of the walls went faster with the added materials. Within a few days, they were about half done and happy with the results so far.

The perimeter alarm sounded early one morning and a reaction team that had already been established went out to meet whoever or whatever was out there. They sent pop up flairs to illuminate the area, and men came from out in front of the bunker across the river that was now a stream again. They fired warning shots, and the intruders all lay down on the ground.

Incoming fire erupted and a firefight ensued. More men came up from the bunker to help and more illumination flares were launched. The marauders were finally driven off after almost an hour, but a security team would have to be left up on the surface until daylight when everything could be assessed.

That morning when the sun came up, the security team could see that about a dozen people had been hit on the other side. Some were still alive, they saw as they went through the field.

"What are we going to do with them?" asked Jake.

"What can we do?" asked Joe.

"Do we just let them die like the man we found on the pole? I won't make that call," said Jake.

"Me either," said Joe.

"Can any of them be saved?" asked Ray as he walked up to them.

"This one was just shot in the leg," said Joe as he walked up to a very dirty man. "What were you doing out here last night?" asked Ray as he turned the man over. The man pointed a handgun at Ray and fired as he rolled over. Jake and Joe opened fire on him and went over to Ray. "You ok buddy?" asked Joe.

"Am I bleeding?" Ray asked the men.

"You caught the round in your body armor," Jake replied.

"You lucky bastard," said Joe as he helped him up.

"Well I guess that answers all our questions. We should just kill them," said Ray.

Steve and a few others came running when they heard the gunfire.

"What happened?" asked James. It was all explained to the rest of them and they decided that they couldn't trust the wounded men. They were left outside as a warning to anyone else that might want to try to harm the people in the bunkers.

Construction of the perimeter was stepped up and finished within days.

With the newly built walls to keep out the marauders, everyone felt better about not having a guard posted out there in the cold.

"How are the revisions coming Joe?" asked Steve.

"I think we will be ready next time."

Once the walls were built, the children were allowed to play in the compound yard as long as they stayed out of the way of those trying to work. The older kids were enlisted to help on certain projects as they were needed.

Some of the women, with Nancy in charge, tried to plant a small garden, but no plants came up. Karen had the idea of starting the plants in the bunker and then putting the small plants outside to continue to grow, but they just died out in the cold nights.

Everyone was taking a break one afternoon and converged on the center of the compound where a few people were already talking.

"We might have to think about moving south," said Simon.

"You're right," said Steve. "It's the middle of July and the nights feel like December. The days aren't as warm as they should be either. We have all we need here, but we can't survive long term here not without proper shelter above ground or planting crops that won't die."

"Do we have enough room in the vehicles to take everything south?" asked Nate.

"That's the problem, we really don't."

"So what do we leave here and what do we take?"

"We will need to take a complete inventory of all we have from this bunker and from the one behind us in the mountainside," said Steve.

"I'm sure that they have gotten into Sanctuary One already and destroyed what we couldn't take," said Joe.

"Not necessarily," said Steve. "It was built to withstand a nuclear attack so they would have to have access to cutting torches and be diligent about it."

"Then we could essentially lock up what we can't take and come back for it right? That may be the only option we have, but will we have enough fuel to do that? How far do we need to go?"

"So should we go south?" asked Trevor.

"South would be the logical choice," said James. "It will be warmer closer to the equator."

"I think we should go west," said Steve.

"Why would we do that?" asked Gary. "I agree with James that south would be the best choice and warmer."

"I have a really strong feeling about west," said Steve.

"Are you sure?" asked Karen.

"West, yes that's where we need to go."

"I would listen to him," said Karen. "He had a feeling like this when he talked us all into building the bunkers."

"Ok," said James, "west it is, but the question is do we go before winter or go in the spring when we will have more travel time?"

James brought up a good question. After spending so much time on the new perimeter walls would they have enough time to get to a warmer place?

It was decided with a large majority vote that the group would stay for the winter and leave in the springtime. Focus was put toward the dike that had been built to divert the water so the hatch could be opened on Sanctuary Three earlier the next year.

"We need to be able to get out when all the snow melts again," said James to everyone as they groaned about the work.

Joe and Jake put out the landmines and tripwires for the claymore mines strategically. They didn't want anyone to get hurt, but the bunker, the supplies and all the people had to be protected.

It took most of the short summer to put the perimeter up and it just kept getting colder. The snow lines on the surrounding mountains were getting lower by the day and it would be snowing on the plains soon.

The mountain supply bunker was secured when the first snow started to fall. The marauders had not been back, and still no Craig either. Everyone had hoped that Craig would come back before winter. More people made the chances of survival better and everyone that occupied the bunkers had been chosen for a reason. Craig was no exception.

The electronic perimeter security, mines and cameras would hopefully be enough to keep people out over the winter if the snow and cold didn't do it all by itself.

Everyone crowded into one bunker and would have to make do over the winter. There were enough rooms for everyone, but the quarters were tight enough for just fourteen people, and now there were thirty-four people with nowhere to go during the day once the hatch was closed for good. It wasn't the best circumstance, but safety in numbers was the logical choice.

James called a meeting in the common area once it was decided to close the hatch for the winter.

"I know no one is looking forward to being down here for months with so many people, but this is the best scenario we could come up with. And it's just a temporary one. As you have all been told, when the snow melts and we have warmer weather we are heading west to start over. We will take as much as we can when we leave and hopefully come back to get more or the rest once we have found a good place to start a civilization. Does anyone have any questions?" asked James. Surprisingly nobody did so James thanked everyone and asked them to check their assignments on the roster.

Maria had teamed up with a few of the other women and opened up a salon in Sanctuary Three. They were cutting and styling hair for the whole group of people now living together. They all did what they could to bring normality to their lives underground.

Jake and Joe went to the armory to double check everything. It was more crowded in there now with a lot of Sanctuary One's gear, weapons and ammo in the way. They could have stored more of it in the mountain bunker, but felt better with it right at their fingertips.

They all went about life just like they did before, but this time they had more help with more people in almost every field of expertise. Steve was on a computer and typing away one day in the common area when Karen walked up to him.

"I just realized in all of the excitement recently, that you haven't been writing in your journal. I haven't read any books lately either," she said.

"I've put it on my laptop," said Steve. "In fact I'm catching up right now. I'll be done soon with the latest chapters if you want to read it."

"I would love that," said Karen. "I'm glad you're writing about all of this. Future generations will know what happened out there and what we had to go through to rebuild our civilization," she said. With that, Karen walked away smiling.

There were meetings all the time about what to take when they left and what routes to take on the road. Sometimes people disagreed, but in the end everything was hammered out.

"We need to take all the battery banks and the windmill parts in the supply bunker so we have electricity when we settle on a good place," said James at one of the meetings.

"I agree with that," said Steve. "And we should bring as much building materials and equipment with us as we can." The two housing vans that were attached to the Kenworth tractors would be filled up with supplies. It was figured that two days on the road without any problems would be fine and everyone could just stay in the Hummers until a good destination was reached.

Springtime was fast approaching and water supplies were being diminished faster than normal with so many people. There was still quite a bit left in the tank, but it was a concern.

The very large group all gathered in the common area for one of the last big meetings before they would leave. Steve and James were at the front of the room.

"You have all been doing a great job given the circumstances," said Steve. "We have a plan that will take us out of this area and to an area that is hopefully a better place to live where we can grow crops and rebuild the human race. We all need to stay optimistic and supportive of one another in the time ahead. I for one believe in all of you. The outside temperature is now above freezing and we will be opening the hatch soon to start getting everything ready to go. Does everyone know what they need to do once we start?"

"Does anyone have any questions?" asked James.

"I do," said Ray. "Where are we going?"

"We are going west," said Steve.

"I know that," said Ray, "but where to? Do we have a destination, or just west?"

"I don't know exactly where yet," said Steve.

"Well it would be nice to know don't you think?" asked Ray. Others agreed, and some still wanted to go south.

"We will have it all figured out before we start down the road," said James.

The following days were spent doing final inventories of everything and packing. Everyone was getting excited about the possibility of getting out and seeing what was left out there in the world, but leery at the same time.

The next week the hatch was opened and no water dumped in as it had the year before. A security team went out first to check the perimeter and mount the machine guns on the towers before anyone else came out. Once the all clear was given, the rest went about their duties. All the vehicles would stay in the supply bunker until they were ready to leave, just in case they were attacked before then. They were loaded up and ready to go within days. The water tanks in the trailers were filled up with the rest of the water from the sanctuary just before it was time to go. The water that was left in Sanctuary Two would be pumped out and put in Sanctuary Three's tank. If things didn't work out for finding a new place to re-build, the group would be back and would need resources. If everything did work out, they could get the water and bring it back on the second trip with the rest of the supplies if they needed to.

One day as Joe was walking the perimeter he came across Jake, who was just staring at a compass.

"What are you doing man?" asked Joe.

"Do you have a compass?" he asked.

"Yes I do, why?"

"That's west that way right?" asked Jake as he pointed.

"It is as far as I know," said Joe.

"Then why does my compass read south?"

"Your compass has to be wrong," said Joe as he pulled his out of its pouch. "Here, mine is brand new," he said as he pointed it where west was. "Mine reads south also," said Joe. "What the hell is going on here?" They both went to find Steve and James to see if they had an answer.

Steve was in the supply bunker when they found him. He knew that his suspicions about the climate change and pole change were correct when the men told him about the compasses. James agreed with Steve.

"The poles have shifted and we are experiencing a climate change on a global scale," said James. "I never thought I would see something like this."

"What do you think caused it?" asked Jake.

"The bombs or the radiation?" asked Joe.

"There is no way to know for sure," said Steve.

Soon everyone knew about the poles being moved and there were a lot of questions that no one could answer for sure.

It was the beginning of May when everyone was ready to go. The security of the compound was ready. The vehicles were outside of the gates and loaded with as much as they could carry.

"So where are we going?" Ray asked Steve.

"Idaho," said Steve, and he walked to the front Humvee to inform them.

"That guy has been acting strange for a while now," Ray said to Nate.

"You're right," said Joe, who was standing by them. "It's like someone has taken control of him. He's not the same Steve all the time"

"I don't care," said Ray, "as long as my family is safe." Everyone got into their assigned vehicles and confirmed radio contact.

Chapter Nineteen: Greener Pastures

Steve told everyone that he had a good feeling about heading toward Lewiston, Idaho or at least that area.

"It is west," said James, "well south really, but not that far south. Are you sure about this?" "Just trust me and you will see," said Steve over the radio. "If we go farther, there might be too much residual radiation because of the large cities on the old west coast."

They decided to put everything essential that couldn't be taken on the first trip inside the mountain bunker. It would be virtually impossible for anyone to get inside. The fuel tanker would stay due to the risk of meeting an enemy on the road with enough firepower to destroy it. The idea for now was to bring enough extra fuel in cans to last for a few weeks of driving and to make a trip back to the sanctuary when necessary.

Jake had the idea to put land mines in front of the bunker doors to protect it, in case anyone got past the perimeter and the walls.

"If they can't get past these," he said while putting them into the ground, "then they can't get in the bunker."

As the convoy rolled out early in the morning, two Hummers in the front and two in the back guarded the two tractors and trailers. With the turrets and machineguns on top of the Hummers, the trailers would be well protected.

No one rode in the trailers; their walls were too susceptible to penetrating bullets. Everyone was in the Hummers with all their armor to protect them.

There was no resistance for the first few miles. The only place that they were worried about was on the road that climbed into the mountains. There were a few choke points in the mountains, and they could be ambushed there.

The convoy stopped within sight of the road as it climbed into the mountains between Craver and Reed Point. Joe got out of his Hummer. Jake got out too and helped him put the UAV they had found in the supply bunker into action. They would have used it the entire way, but with so much flat ground and no vegetation, it wasn't necessary.

The UAV was ready and Joe started it by throwing it up into the air like a paper airplane. Jake manned the controls while Joe watched the video screen.

"Keep climbing," he told Jake.

"Switch to thermal," said Joe. "I see movement on top of that next rise."

"We can take two motorcycles and sniper rifles to take them out," said Jake. "How many do you see?"

"Around thirty," said Joe.

"Are you kidding me?" asked Jake. "Where the hell did they come from?"

"I like your idea of using sniper rifles," said Joe, "but we should send two Hummers as well for support."

"I like your thinking," said Jake. Joe had drawn a map of the area for them to go off of by viewing the UAV's flight on the monitor. Jake turned the UAV around. The guys all got together to decide the plan of attack. They would only fire if fired upon first. These rules of engagement were agreed on by everyone.

The plan came together rather quickly and everyone understood their individual parts. Joe and Jake took the ramp down off the back of the lead trailer and got out two motor cycles. They took them off road and headed for a hill adjacent to the one they had seen the heat signatures on. The two support Hummers continued up the highway to draw the marauders out for the snipers to deal with.

The men in the vehicles made contact with Joe and Jake. The two men let them know when they were set up. As the Hummers approached the choke point, Joe told them to stop.

"What's happening?" asked Ray, who was driving the lead Hummer.

"They're being attacked from their left flank," said Jake.

"Who is attacking them?" asked Steve.

"Its Craig guys!" yelled Joe. "It's got to be!"

"We are going hot here to support him. Keep your distance and we'll let you know when you can proceed," said Jake.

The two men fired at targets almost a mile away as they moved out of Craig's firing line. The thirty plus men were taken out within minutes. Joe and Jake could see a lone man, more than likely Craig, walking around and finishing off the wounded. Joe told the two Hummer operators that all hostiles were down, but to proceed with extreme caution. The Hummers rolled up the road and were met by a lone man standing in the middle. He was very dirty and had many weapons hanging off his body. It was Craig. He had a long beard and his hair was getting long too.

Steve got out to talk to him, and Craig started to walk toward him. Nate was on the lead Hummers machine gun turret. He pointed the .50 cal mounted on top the vehicle at Craig before he realized who he was.

"I wouldn't do that if I were you boy," said Craig in a tone that made Nate shiver. Nate pointed the machine gun to the left flank and apologized to Craig.

"Where have you been Craig?" asked Steve.

"I went hunting," said Craig.

"For six months?" asked Steve.

"Well it took me awhile to find my prey."

"What have you been eating and drinking and where did you stay this past winter?" asked Steve.

"All good questions," said Craig. "For now can we just get on the road to paradise please? I'm tired, hungry and need a shower. I see you brought two of my mobile living quarters. Good thinking, they will come in handy." With that, Craig got into the second Hummer, just as Joe and Jake rode up.

"What did he tell you?" asked Joe.

"He is glad to be back and needs a shower," said Steve as he walked away.

"Did you ask him where he has been and how he survived?" asked Jake.

"I did," said Steve, "and he'll tell us later. Now let's get back to the others and get on down the road."

The two Hummers and two motorcycles turned around and headed back to the rest of the convoy. When they got there, everyone wanted to know what happened. The returning men told them that they would find out soon. Craig got out of one of the Hummer's, much to everyone's surprise, and went directly up the ramp into the trailer. He took off his gear and started to take off his clothes. At that point, Steve closed the doors and put the ramp back under the trailer.

"Joe, Jake, will you ride those things for a while longer?" he asked them.

"You bet we will," said Jake. The two motorcycles would follow the convoy so they wouldn't be vulnerable if they came under attack. The vehicles all started down the road again and within an hour the tractor and trailer behind the lead Hummer started to leak some kind of fluid.

Kyle was driving the tractor.

"Kyle, this is Ray," he said over the radio.

"Go ahead," said Kyle.

"I see something leaking out of the trailer. I recommend that we stop and check it out."

Joe got on the radio. "Wait a minute guys and I'll take a closer look, just keep going for now," he said. Joe rode his motorcycle up beside the trailer and looked under it. "I think Craig is just taking a shower guys," he said.

A few people were laughing over the radio. Steve got on. "He did say he needed one. Let's just keep on going," he said.

The convoy pushed on through the mountains toward Bozeman. The water from Craig's shower soon stopped. The three-hour drive took longer with debris all over the road; it had to be cleared before the tractors could get through. If it was just the Hummers, they could just drive over most of the stuff in the road. The group passed by a few houses along the road that hadn't burned down, but not many. There was no reason to stop, because they had all they needed and didn't want to risk an attack by anyone that might want it. The small towns between the two cities showed no sign of life either as they rolled by on Highway 90. By midafternoon, they were within a few miles of Bozeman. Jake got on the radio as the convoy stopped. "Me and Joe should ride ahead cautiously and scout the road before the city," he said. Everyone agreed it was a good idea and they continued down the road. When the trucks stopped, Craig opened up the man door at the rear of the trailer and jumped out.

"What the hell did we stop for?" he asked.

James walked up to him. "We're close to Bozeman," he said, "and we sent some scouts ahead to make sure the road is clear and no one is waiting to kill us." Craig had shaved his head and cut off his long beard. And after taking a shower, he looked almost normal again, except for the stare he now had. He had lost a lot of weight and was once again ready for action. He called himself, a "Lean mean fighting machine!"

The men on the motorcycles slowed down and stopped as they got within a mile of Bozeman. They radioed back and told the others about the destruction that was laid out before them. Everything looked good enough to bring the others up. Jake made the call and they started down the road. The rest of the vehicles came up behind them and everyone got out to get a better view.

"My god," said Karen as she walked up to the front of the convoy.

"Is this what we are to expect from now on?" asked Maria. "Did every city get bombed?

"There is no way to be certain," said Steve.

"We might want to fly the UAV around and make sure we won't run into any surprises down there," said Joe.

"Good idea," said James.

Jake helped Joe with setting up the equipment and launching the small plane. The two men were getting good at working together. As the UAV flew over the city, not much of any consequence was found. They planned to search a few areas as they drove through, but no one was holding their breath about finding anyone alive. Luckily, Highway 90 didn't travel through the heart of the city and much of it could be bypassed. After the UAV was recovered, the group decided to send two Hummers ahead of the tractors to make sure the entire road was clear. A small group went into the city, which was mainly flattened and scattered around the area. The road was either gone, in some areas completely, or pretty rough, but they figured that the tractors and trailers could make it. Just past where Main Street would have been, there was a large concentration of vehicles covering the road in both directions. The two Hummers stopped and the men got out to assess the area.

"We can move a lot of these today," said Jake, "but we'll have to finish tomorrow unless it continues to be blocked further ahead."

"I say we move what we can now and bring the UAV back to look ahead in the morning," said Craig. James got on the radio and asked Joe to find a good place to spend the night and said they would be back before dark. The men got to work and made a large dent in the vehicles covering the highway. They all took turns sitting in the turret of one of the Hummers to watch the area. They left just before dark to make it back to everyone else.

The night was quiet and passed without incident. The next morning, the convoy continued down the road after a meal of MREs. "At least we have food," Craig told everyone as he saw all their faces when the meals were brought out. After everyone was finished, they all got in the trucks to continue on down the road. The plan was to have the tractors and trailers and two Humvees park at a turn out closer to the traffic jam in order for everyone to be closer. They would be ready to go once the road was clear.

"The first thing we need to do is get the UAV in the air," said Craig as they got back to the traffic jam. Everyone exchanged strange looks and just kept doing what they knew needed to be done. Jake got the UAV out of the Hummer and launched it. Joe was on the monitor to assist as he had been. The little plane flew up and gained altitude. The highway could be seen for miles.

"It looks like there are about twenty more vehicles and then we can continue on," said Joe.

"I wonder why all these trucks were parked only on this part of the road?" asked Jake as he brought the UAV back to earth.

"All of you just stay alert," said Craig. "I don't like this at all. You scanned the entire area son?" Craig asked Joe.

"I saw nothing odd about the view when it passed over the area," said Joe, "and it flew over a large area." Craig walked away toward the end of the traffic jam.

"I take it he isn't helping?" asked James. The rest of the men continued to move the trucks out of the way so they could drive through. They were just about done when Craig walked up to the Hummers and stopped.

"Did you find or see anything?" Joe asked.

"No, all clear up ahead except for that rather large dump I left along the side of the road. Took a while, but it was the best one I have taken in months! You boys ready to go yet?" asked Craig as he walked back to the trailer.

"Is this guy just messing with us, or did those six months away really screw him up?" asked Nate.

"We don't know for sure," said James, "but he isn't the same Craig I used to know. Let's get these last two out of the way and get out of here."

The convoy was soon on the road again, but had to go slow with debris scattered around the highway. A road trip that would normally have taken just over eight hours was on its second day, and the whole group was getting uncomfortable in the vehicles. The next leg of the trip would take them by Butte. It was only seventy miles away, but the sun was going down. James suggested that they go as far as they could before dark and find a good place to stop for the night. They would continue on in the morning, but he didn't like the idea of getting stuck on the road in the middle of the night. Everyone agreed that they would stop at the next turn out or rest area that could be defended well.

The group was tired and glad to stop to rest. A perimeter had to be established before they could. MREs were handed out for dinner. No one complained anymore and knew it was just a matter of time before a real meal could be cooked.

The night was uneventful and everyone got some much needed rest. After another MRE in the morning, they were ready to continue. They still hadn't encountered any other vehicles on the road. There were survivors out there, they knew this, but they had already encountered too many as far as they were concerned.

The convoy would drive right by Butte as long as the road was clear. From there, they would head north toward Missoula, which was now west according to the compass.

Interstate 90 was clear for the most part and the convoy drove right by Butte. Some wondered if anyone was alive, since it looked like all of the buildings were intact.

"If confrontation can be avoided," said Steve "then it will be." The convoy stopped just past Clinton because of debris on the road, which had to be cleared. Some wanted to get out, but were told to stay in the vehicles.

"A random pile of trash or vehicles blocking the road means someone wants to stop you and take your shit," Craig said over the radio. The highway was cleared and the trucks started rolling again.

"We are getting close to Missoula," said James over the radio. The road ahead was clear, so they kept going. They could see smoke rising in different areas as they approached.

The convoy stopped on the outskirts of Missoula. Everyone got out of the vehicles to stretch their legs and to set up a hasty defensive perimeter. Steve got out and turned on the Geiger counter, as he had done every step of the way, to take a reading.

"Still looking good?" asked James.

"It has barely registered since we left," said Steve. "But I'll continue to check as we go, just to be safe." Joe got the UAV from the trailer and Jake helped him set it up. It had become a very handy tool along the way. No one cared to ask how Craig was able to get ahold of a "Switchblade." The US Army had started using them in 2011. This was a more advanced one than they would have seen on TV or read about. The flight time in its fuel cells was almost two hours, so it could cover many miles before having to be turned around. What the group had was better than gold to anyone out there, and had to be protected.

The UAV was ready to launch. Joe sent it up and set its flight path to circle the city. There were almost two hundred thousand people in this area before the bombs fell. Fires had ravaged most of the forests along the way from Billings, so they wouldn't be able to tell anything for sure until the area was reconnoitered.

"You boys are getting pretty good with my little toy," said Craig.

"Thanks," said Jake. "I have actually operated a UAV before, when I was in the Army."

"Well at least you served," Craig said as he walked away.

"He's been a little strange since he got back to the group," said Joe.

"A little?" said Jake smiling.

As the "Switchblade" flew over the city, Joe swapped from standard view to thermal in order to get a better view of any life down below. He could usually distinguish between people or animals and other types of heat signatures.

"Anything yet?" asked Steve.

"I have seen a few large hot spots," said Joe. "Other than that nothing real small, but...wait a minute here we go! I see one, two, no, five small heat signatures in a building that are more than likely people."

"What area of the city?" asked James as he got out a map.

"Southwest in what is probably a warehouse," said Joe. "Jake can you circle around that same area and bring it to a lower altitude?" Jake maneuvered the UAV to where Joe wanted it.

"They are coming out of the building, they must hear it," said Joe. "I see gun fire! Evasive maneuvers!" yelled Joe. Jake banked and climbed as fast as the little plane would go.

"Let's keep it a little higher as you continue," said Craig. "That's the only one of those puppies I could get."

"Roger that," said Jake.

"I have the building marked on the map," said James. A few more areas had what appeared to have human heat signatures and were marked on the map also. Jake turned the little UAV around and brought it back safely.

"Not very many people again," commented Kim.

"You have to remember," reminded Ray, "if they weren't killed in the initial blasts, then they probably died from radiation sickness or died at the hands of marauders, or starvation."

"I know, but I am just hoping every day that my sister and her family are still out there," she said.

"If they are, then we will find them," Steve reassured her as he walked up.

The sun was going down and it would soon be dark, so the designated reaction team went to work on the nighttime perimeter, after a suitable area was chosen to spend the night. They would skirt the city the next morning and hope that all went well.

Just before any daylight could be seen on the horizon, Ray was dozing off again when something crossed a trip wire and a pop up flare launched. Two hundred yards from where Ray sat in one of the Hummer's gun turrets, illuminated by the flare, stood dozens of people. They started running at the vehicles and Ray froze. Jake opened up with a SAW from one of the other turrets and Ray snapped out of his daze and started shooting too. Three more flares were launched from different areas around the perimeter and Jake turned his turret accordingly. The two other Hummers started firing as well. Craig, Steve, Kyle and James came out of the back trailer while putting their gear on and eventually started shooting. Craig popped more flares as the first ones died down. The blinding muzzle flash and the popping of the flares made everything look like it was in slow motion. The people just kept coming, no one wondering why, they just kept shooting and literally blowing them to pieces.

After about ten minutes of almost constant firing, Steve yelled, "Cease fire!" The guns slowly died and they could hear some of the kids screaming. They had woken up to the sound of the battle and it scared them, along with a few of the women. The gunners were told to reload and use night vision and thermal to check the perimeter until the sun came up.

The sun came up about an hour later and showed a horrific scene, laid out all around the convoy. Hundreds of bodies had been cut to pieces by the machine guns. The women and children were told to stay in the vehicles and not to look outside. The men on the ground walked through the bodies to see if anyone was still alive, but none were. The damage that the .50 cals did alone would leave no one alive. A path was cleared so the convoy could move to another location and get everyone away from the massacre. As they drove down the road, the lead Hummer spotted a few people walking in the middle of the road. Some were bloody and limping. Steve stopped his Hummer and got out with cover from the turret gunner, Nate. The injured people stopped and turned around. One man fell to the ground and died right there.

"What were you people doing this morning at our camp?" asked Steve cautiously.

"We are starving," said a woman who looked very sick.

James walked up with a Geiger counter, and it started showing radiation levels that he didn't like. "Steve we need to go now!" James warned.

"I'm sorry," said Steve to the people as James pulled him away. They got back in their vehicles and the convoy moved past Missoula before stopping an hour later.

They pulled over at a scenic lookout and pointed the machine guns outward. No one was talking except Craig of course.

"Well I don't know about anyone else, but I am hungry!"

Nate had had enough and got down off the turret he was on and moved toward Craig.

"You son of a bitch!" he said. "Don't you have a soul? We killed all of those people and just left them!" yelled Nate. Joe and Ray were holding him back as Craig walked up to him and spoke calmly.

"This is war boy and whether you like it or not you saved lives this morning! You remember this! They were going to kill, rape, mutilate every last one of us and maybe even eat us! We are all on the same side, the winning side! Now you stow your damn emotions and act like a man!" Craig walked away and Nate just stood there not knowing what to do. He knew Craig was right, but had to work through it.

After a perimeter was established, the group got together and Steve reassured them.

"I know these last couple of years have been hard on everyone, but the thing we need to keep in mind is that we are still alive. We have overcome more than most of you thought we could. We will make it to a place where we can start again. We have to continue to work together and we will survive. We will rest here for a day, eat some real hot food and continue on in the morning." They all helped out to get the meal ready and Nate walked up to Craig. All eyes were watching them, not knowing what might happen.

"I just wanted to say," started Nate.

"You can do it son," said Craig.

"You were right," said Nate. "I am sorry, I lost it."

"If that is the worst thing you do, I welcome it," grinned Craig. Nate reached out his hand to shake Craig's. Craig grabbed him and gave him a hug. "I'm proud of you son!" said Craig with admiration. They sat down to eat a meal that had been cooked instead of one from a plastic bag.

The most direct route would have taken them through the heart of the city, but there was no way through according to what they saw from the UAV camera. The only way was all the way around by back tracking on highway 474 and then across to the 263. From there, they could get to highway 12. This was the best route, but it would take them through a few large neighborhoods. The journey was split up into small legs with stops to fly ahead with the UAV. If there was a roadblock or debris across the highway they would try to use a different way to get around.

The group would leave the next morning and would try to push past Lolo before stopping for the night. This was a rural area and there would be less chance of people attacking them.

With some minor detours, the convoy made it safely to a ranch just off the road past Lolo. The house and out buildings were searched, but they found no one. All the structures were intact, but no one was home. Many things were missing; there were no vehicles either.

"They must have left to find a better place," Maria said to Kim.

"There is no way to tell anything for sure," said Nancy.

A perimeter was established around the house and Steve and James swept the entire area with the Geiger counters before everyone got settled inside. Joe and Jake put out the usual trip wires with flares for security.

The next day after collecting all the trip wires and flares, the convoy moved out toward Lolo Hot Springs and a winding road through the mountains. The drive through what used to be a vast wilderness was now just a large burned area that looked like it was a thousand years old. Once through the mountains, they stopped in a large open area on the side of the road on the Montana and Idaho border before the final push toward Lewiston.

Chapter Twenty :
Unbelievable

It had been a very long trip, one that should have taken just over eight hours in a normal world. Everyone was tired and ready for it to be over. Craig reminded them that they had it easy compared to most other people in the world. "You have food, water and shelter," he said one night. The nights were growing warmer as they headed toward Lewiston and it made everyone feel better about Steve's choice of direction.

It was early on the fifth morning when De Novo, the new addition to the group, woke the entire trailer up.

"What's wrong with him?" Steve asked Karen as he turned on a light above their bed in the trailer.

"I don't know, this is the first time he has woken up this early, and never crying," said Karen.

Gary walked over and asked if they wanted him to look at the baby.

"Yes, could you?" asked Karen.

Gary took him to the dining table and pulled it down off the wall. "Now, what is wrong with you little guy?" Gary asked as he pushed on the baby's stomach and pressed here and there. The baby stopped crying and just stared at Gary.

"What do you think?" asked Karen.

"He seems to be fine," said Gary. "I guess he just wanted us all to get up."

The people in the trailer slowly got up and turned lights on. It was only five in the morning, but an early start would get them that much closer to their destination.

Steve got on the radio and asked James, "How do things look out there this morning?"

"No activity last night of course," said James. "I hope we can gain more ground today."

"I hope we can get all the way to Lewiston," commented Jake on the radio. "I feel like I'm back in Iraq and don't know when I will get to the next FOB."

"Quit your bitching," said Craig. "This is nothing like combat! We haven't had anyone shoot directly at us the whole trip."

No one had much energy that morning and moved slowly. It was late morning before they were all ready to get back on the road. The drive through the mountains could prove to be a treacherous one. With all of the trees burned down, the chance of mud slides and parts of the highway being washed away was great. The UAV would once again be put into action. This of course meant multiple launches, recoveries and recharging of the fuel cells. The hope was to get past Kamiah at least.

Joe and Jake rode ahead on the motor cycles with a small chain saw to clear any trees across the road. The convoy would stay back a mile or two just in case there was any trouble ahead. They would hopefully be able to turn around, but most areas of the road were too narrow to allow a tractor with the trailer to accomplish this.

Joe rode slightly ahead of Jake and they both hoped that nothing had been put across the road, like a rope or wire. They could potentially be cut in half if there was. They agreed that it would not be a good thing to happen. The trip was a slow one with them being as cautious as they were. Joe turned on a curve in the road and stopped. Jake saw him and stopped next to him.

Joe got on the radio. "We have a few trees in the road," he said. "Can you send the lead Hummer to cover us while we clear the road?"

"On our way," said Steve.

The rest of the convoy would stay right where they were until they were told to proceed. Jake went to work with the chainsaw and Joe moved the logs over the edge of the embankment. Within a few minutes, the trees were cleared out of the road.

"Looks like a good place to launch the Switchblade," said Craig. Joe and Jake went over to the Hummer to get some water and take a break. Craig ran the UAV above the winding road for miles with the standard camera, then turned on the thermal on the way back. "Looks clear for miles," said Craig. He recovered the UAV and the convoy was told to move up.

Jake took off down the road and Joe followed him. The men pushed on with the convoy close behind. They passed a sign that said, "Welcome to Kamiah," and they relayed their progress on the radio. They passed houses and other structures along the road. As they turned another corner Joe yelled over the radio, "Everyone stop!"

The convoy stopped where they were. "You guys can come up here where we are," Jake said. The rest of the vehicles slowly moved up to where the two motorcycles were and stopped.

No one could believe what they were seeing. The scorched earth just stopped as they came out of the mountains and lush, green trees and bushes were laid out in front of them for as far as they could see.

"Do you have any idea why the burn stopped here and left all of that alone?" James asked Steve as he pointed ahead.

"No idea at all," said Steve. They were still about forty miles from Lewiston, but it was like they were on a different planet.

"This is a good sign right?" asked Nancy. "We haven't seen any wildlife the whole way except for a few birds."

"A very good one," said Craig, walking up beside Nancy and startling her. The entire group had gotten out to admire the scenery and no one was watching the surrounding area.

"If there are trees and other vegetation then there should still be insects and wildlife," said Simon. "Yes Nancy, Craig is right. This is a very good sign. This means that there should be other areas around the globe that have survived too. The earth will heal itself and will continue on."

A man walked up from behind them and said, "Isn't it beautiful?" The group started to turn around and those with guns pointed them at him. "No need to get violent," said the man. "I just heard the trucks and thought I would come have a look see is all. Marge and I haven't heard one on this road in years. I can go back home now if you don't want to talk."

"Where did you come from?" asked Steve.

"My house is right up this drive. I can show you if you would like," said the man. He was pointing and shaking. Craig walked up to him.

"You nervous about something old man?" asked Craig.

"The shaking, oh that's just the palsy that's all. Would you like to come up to the house?" he asked again.

"Let me talk to my friends for a minute," Craig said. He motioned for the rest of the guys to come over to him and whispered, "There's something strange about this guy and I think we should leave. What's he doing now Nate?"

"He keeps looking to his left."

"Ok, this is what we are going to do," said Craig. "I will walk back up to him and as soon as I grab him and turn him around, I want you guys with no weapons to grab the women and kids and get to cover. The rest of you open fire on the brush he keeps looking at." Craig walked back up to the old man and said, "Ok let's go to your place. Lead the way." The man turned around with a smile on his face and Craig grabbed him around the neck. He then kicked his legs out from underneath him and put him on his knees. Craig used him as a shield until the man lost consciousness. The bushes opened up with muzzle flashes and the others fired back. Joe jumped up on the closest hummer and started firing the .50 cal and mowed down the brush and the people shooting at them. The women and children got to cover with none of them getting shot. Ray was grazed by a bullet on his left upper thigh and Kyle took one in his shoulder. "Move and get in the trucks!" Craig yelled. Everyone followed his direction quickly.

They convoy sped away down the road. Nate was in the last Hummer, manning the turret and shooting until they turned a corner and he couldn't see the area any longer.

"This is Steve, do we have everyone?" he asked over the radio. All of them were accounted for. "We will stop in a few miles once we see a good area to pull over where that won't happen again," he said.

"Was anyone shot?" asked Gary.

"This is Kyle. I was shot in the shoulder."

"We'll look at it just as soon as we stop, just keep pressure on it," said Trevor.

"I got shot in the leg."

"Who is this?" asked Gary.

"It's Ray, who else?"

"You need to say your name," said Craig. "He can't see you."

"Same thing," said Trevor. "Just keep pressure on it."

"This is Ray again, and I will keep pressure on it." A clear pull out was just up ahead and they all pulled over.

Craig got out of his Hummer and started barking orders. "I want the Hummers to flank the tractor and trailer," he said. "You men in the gunner seats keep scanning the area and let me know if you see any movement. I want the wounded to get in the trailer and have the docs fix you up." Everyone complied and no one questioned him.

"He's back," Jake said over the radio.

"He sure is," said Joe.

"I want radio silence unless you have something tactically important to say," Craig said in a stern voice.

The two wounded men got into the trailer and the doctors, Gary and Trevor, checked them out. Ray wasn't even bleeding anymore, so Trevor told him to, wait there until they checked on Kyle, and he went to assist Gary. Kyle had a small caliber wound to the left rear part of his upper shoulder.

"Bite on this cloth," Gary told Kyle. Gary reached into the wound with a pair of tweezers as Kyle screamed into the cloth, and pulled out a .32 caliber bullet. "All done," Gary said. "Let us just wash out the wound and sew you up."

"You were lucky someone had a small handgun instead of a rifle pointed at you," said Craig.

Trevor went back over to Ray and cleaned out his wound. He put a butterfly bandage on it and said, "Unless it starts bleeding again we won't use any stitches."

Gary told both men to keep their wounds clean. They would only take a course of antibiotics if they got infected. With no way to replenish the small supply of meds they had, they would only use them if they really needed too.

The group was asked to meet in the middle of the convoy. The men on the turrets would listen on the radio. Steve kept his mike open for them to hear.

"That was a close call back there," said Steve. "If you don't know it by now, we have been very lucky this whole trip. We have had it so good for so long, that we are not in the right state of mind. The world that we knew is gone. A new untamed world now exists. People are hungry, desperate and want everything we have including our lives. We will put some more distance between us and the farm where we were ambushed and before we spend the night. With any more luck, we will reach Lewiston sometime tomorrow." They all got back in the trucks and drove down the road a few more miles. They found a nice open area with a clear view of the tree line on all sides.

Craig put together the reaction team this time. Steve mentioned to James how it appeared that they had the old Craig back.

"The man has been through hell," said James. The two men continued on helping to get ready for the night.

"I want claymores set up with trip wires in these areas on the inner perimeter," said Craig as he pointed at his drawn out map on the ground. The flares will trip first and then if they keep coming, the claymores will take them out. I don't want anyone to make it past the wire. Those of you on the turret guns, hold your fire until I give the order unless it looks like we might be overrun."

"Do you think we'll be attacked again?" asked Nate.

"Son, let me tell you, all of you," said Craig. "Being prepared for anything to happen will allow you to react much faster and you will win the fight. Never bring a knife to a gunfight, never get within arm's length of anyone if you can avoid it and last but not least, never pick a fistfight with an old man, because he knows he can't win so he will just kill you. Everyone got it?" he asked. "Now get to work and don't blow yourselves up."

All of the women and kids slept in the trailers along with Kyle and Ray.

They both wanted to stand guard with the rest of the men, but Gary told them both, "The faster you heal up, the faster you can help out again." The night dragged on. With the claymore mines in place, Craig let the security fall to fifty percent after midnight. At about two a.m., a flare popped up.

Craig spoke softly over the radio. "Nobody move," he said. The flare died down. A few minutes later, in the same direction, a claymore exploded. Craig popped a flare and the men on that side could see a cloud of dust. "Keep watching," said Craig. As soon as the flare burned out, he popped another one and they could see about a dozen people crawling in toward the vehicles.

"Light 'em up!" yelled Craig. The machine guns ripped the men to shreds. In the trailer, everyone woke up and could hear the .50 cal thumping away, and then the smaller machine guns answering back. "Cease fire, cease fire!" yelled Craig over the radio. "North side, give me a sit rep," said Craig.

"All clear over here," said Joe.

"Everyone stay alert," said Craig. "We will assess the damage in the daylight."

The remainder of the morning was calm. As soon as the sun came up, Craig, Steve and Jake walked over to the area of penetration. They found about eight bodies in a small area.

"Follow me in a straight line," said Craig.

"What do you see?" asked Jake.

"A blood trial," said Craig. The men followed behind Craig through the woods and past the perimeter. Craig stopped and put his hand up. He motioned for the men to move to his left and right. As soon as they got on line, they slowly moved forward. Behind a dead fall lay two men, and a third was crawling away. The first two had bled out. They approached the third man. Jake rolled him over and the man spit up blood.

"What do you want?" he asked. "Just kill me and get it over with."

"Did you come from that farm down the road?" asked Steve.

"What if I did?"

"Why did you attack us?" asked Craig.

"We wanted your women and food, why else?" said the man laughing. Craig took out his .45 1911 and put a round between his eyes.

"Why did you do that?" asked Steve. "He could have told us more."

"He was done talking. He was dead and he knew it." Craig started walking back to the convoy.

When the three men got back, breakfast was almost done. Steve told the group that everything was ok. After breakfast, the trip wires on the perimeter and the rest of the claymores were picked up. The convoy started down the road toward Lewiston and hopefully a new start.

The road looked clear, but they drove slowly just in case. They were about fifteen miles away once they crossed the last bridge over the Clear Water River, before North Lewiston came into view. With the mountains in the way, they would have to get closer to get the UAV up in the air for a better view. When they could see the power plant on the other side of the river, they knew they were close enough to launch the UAV and cover most of the city.

They pulled over on a bypass road. A few men stayed in the turrets of the Hummers just in case, but they could see for a long way up and down the road and felt safe enough to let everyone out. As the Switchblade was prepped for its flight, they all walked around. Finally, the anticipation was over.

"We are ready to launch," Jake said.

With Joe manning the monitor, Jake launched the UAV. It gained altitude and they guided it toward the city.

It flew over the power plant first. "Guys am I seeing people down there?" Joe asked.

A few of the others crowded around the small monitor.

"They look like they are working down there," said Steve.

""Circle around again," said James. Jake made another pass and saw they were right.

"Head toward the city now," said Craig.

Jake flew the Switchblade over downtown Lewiston and saw people everywhere.

"This can't be," said James. "The city is surrounded by vegetation, there are no radiation signatures above normal, and there are people all over the place. How could this be possible?" Jake continued to fly the UAV over the rest of the city and they saw even more people walking around, but no moving vehicles.

The group talked about what to do with the information they had. Jake landed the UAV and joined the conversation.

"We should be very careful here," said Craig. "With so many people we could be overrun if they want all of this." He pointed toward the vehicles.

"I agree," said Steve. "We should send a scout vehicle."

Craig, Nate, Steve and James were the best choices to go and find out if it was safe, while the rest would stay back to protect the convoy. As the scout Hummer got almost parallel across the river from the power plant, the men could see a huge road block.

They stopped. "What should we do?" James asked.

Craig looked through his binoculars. "I see dozens of armed men out there on the wall," he said. They decided that the worst thing that could happen would be the men wouldn't let them in, but then, they could just open fire on them too. Nate pointed the .50 cal to the rear. Steve got out and put a white t-shirt on the communications antenna and they drove slowly toward the heavily armed road block.